THE
BAD BELL
OF
SAN
SALVADOR

THE
BAD BELL
OF
SAN
SALVADOR

PATRICIA BEATTY

frontispiece by Ben F. Stahl
William Morrow and Company
New York 1973

Printed in the United States of America.

Library of Congress Catalog Card Number: 73-4921

1 2 3 4 5 77 76 75 74 73

CONTENTS

THE
BAD BELL
OF
SAN
SALVADOR

THE
HOUSE
OF
DELACRUZ

I

Wherever he was, whatever he was doing, Jacinto the Comanche always stopped to hear the bells whose music he heard throughout Santa Fe. He delighted in their differing voices.

Now he stood listening in the courtyard of Don Hilario's house, leaning on the rake with which he was clearing leaves and twigs from the garden canal. In his mind he identified the bells of the Church of Saint Francis. The bells of the Chapel of San Miguel had rung earlier and fallen silent. Each day began for Jacinto with his hearing the matin call from one Santa Fe church, and each ended with the lovely "Ave Maria" from the copper bells of another.

And as far as thirteen-year-old Jacinto was concerned, the bells were the only pleasant thing he'd found in any church in Santa Fe. Try as they would, no New Mexican, not even his *patrón*, Don Hilario Delacruz, was going to make a Christian of him. They could name him Jacinto, but that was not his name. He was Spotted Wild Horse, a Comanche Indian of the band known as Honey Eaters.

When the bells of the Church of Saint Francis had finished ringing, Jacinto went back reluctantly to clearing the canal. But his ears were still so filled with the memory of their beautiful sound that he didn't hear Esperanza when she began calling to him.

Her voice had risen to a shout before he looked up from his work. "You, Jacinto, come here. Come at once. Pronto," shrilled the voice he detested above all others.

Jacinto straightened up, rake in hand, and slowly turned his head to glare at the fat woman in the doorway of Don Hilario's kitchen. She was frowning at him, puffing at the *cigarrito* between her teeth. Still holding the rake, he came slowly toward her, noticing with satisfaction how Don Hilario's housekeeper tapped her foot on the flagstones.

Removing her *cigarrito*, Esperanza snapped, "Pronto! Move more swiftly, stupid one. What, you have not finished with the canal yet? And you have still to give water to the flowers in the window boxes. Then you are to take a donkey and go to the wood sellers in

Burro Alley. Buying this wood is the order of the *patrón* himself." Esperanza put her hand into her apron pocket, pulled out two silver reales, and shoved them into a fold of the sash around the boy's waist. Then she went back into the kitchen to enjoy her *cigarrito*, slamming the door behind her to let Jacinto know what she thought of him.

Quickly Jacinto finished his work on the canal, then splashed water from a pail into the window boxes. He dropped the pail with a crash onto the courtyard flagstones and ran for the stables. Only the bells of Santa Fe and his *patrón*'s stables were worth his time. The stables, when he could have them to himself, were a haven of happiness. Like every other gentleman, Don Hilario kept many horses, fine ones of the "blood of Spanish barbs, not Indian ponies," as Esperanza said.

The boy opened the stable door and slid into the gloom, sniffing the scent of horses with joy. Before he untied a donkey he'd visit Don Hilario's favorite mount, a chestnut stallion of great beauty. Jacinto went into the stallion's stall, murmuring to him in Comanche, patting his neck. How he wished he could ride this horse. As a Comanche, Jacinto knew he could ride better than Donato Delacruz, Don Hilario's son. Comanche children were tied onto the back of a pony before they could even walk. A boy of six had his own pony. What did these New Mexicans know of horses? Nothing.

"Someday soon I will take you, god-dog," Jacinto whispered into the ear of the chestnut. "Then I will ride you eastward out onto the plains and find my father's people. You will be a great chief among the god-dogs of the Comanches, the horse of Spotted Wild Horse, who stole you from the house of an enemy."

Jacinto glared at the heavy silver-mounted saddle and bridle thrown over the top of the chestnut's stall. What did any Delacruz know of horses? A Comanche didn't need a saddle at all, only a pad of buffalo skin. As for bridles, Jacinto scowled, looking at the long metal bit that went into the chestnut's mouth. It was a Spanish bit, the most cruel of all. Comanche ponies never had metal shoved into their mouth. They had only halters of braided buffalo hair.

Jacinto gave the chestnut a final pat on his sleek neck and went to untie the mouse-gray donkey-of-all-work. Putting a halter and ropes on the animal was only an instant's work, and the boy did so with disgust. Donkeys had no spirit, only endurance and stubbornness. Comanches ate donkeys and mules but did not ride such low animals. Jacinto went sourly out of the Delacruz stable, leading the little donkey, wishing it were a horse.

As he started for the Plaza and Burro Alley, Jacinto thought of the years he'd spent in the Delacruz household. They had been hard years of shameful housework and garden work done under the orders of a woman.

They had been years of lectures from Don Hilario and from old Padre Luna, of the Chapel of San Miguel, whose duty it was to make a Christian out of a Comanche. And then there always had been the teasing and tormenting of Donato and his slim olive-skinned sisters, who laughed at Jacinto's stockiness and broad face and said that his skin was the color of an "old copper cooking pot." According to the haughty Donato, all Comanches were ugly and needed *disciplina*, the Spanish word for *whip*.

Approaching the Plaza of Santa Fe, the boy recalled the first time he'd seen it. He'd been only ten years old, but he'd put up a good fight all the same, squirming on the horse held by the Mexican who'd captured him. He scowled thinking of the name Jacinto that he'd been given in Santa Fe. Like all names given to New Mexican children, it was a Christian saint's name and in his case a holy martyr's name. But *jacinto* meant *hyacinth*, and a hyacinth, he'd learned, was a *flower*! What sort of joke was that, to name a Comanche boy who was a chief's son after a flower?

It was near sunset now. Trust old Esperanza to wait until the last moment to send him after firewood. He'd better hurry or he might feel the *disciplina* on his back again. Jacinto pulled hard on the donkey's rope as they went down the mud street into the Plaza. Then quickly he had to leap aside as a man on a horse came trotting past him, heading for the Plaza fence where he would tether it. The horseman, a *caballero*, would have ridden Jacinto down under his horse's hooves without a second thought. That was the way of horsemen. Jacinto looked enviously after the man, marking the velvet jacket and silver spurs as the *caballero* dismounted and went along the walk that surrounded the Plaza on three sides under overhanging balconies. The *caballero* went into La Fonda, Santa Fe's finest inn—more than likely to gamble, the boy thought.

Jacinto passed the Palace of the Governors, the long adobe building on the north side of the Plaza. Already candlelight gleamed behind the glass windows, but now at dusk there were no Indians here selling their corns and scarlet strings of dried peppers. They'd all gone back to their villages and would return the next day to squat before the Palace again. Jacinto always laughed to himself with contempt when he thought of these Indians. They were Pueblos. What kind of Indians were they? Farmers—farmers who lived on top of one another in houses made of mud.

Mud! Santa Fe itself was made of mud. The streets were of mud. Save for its cottonwood trees, picket fence, and metal sundial, the Plaza was mud. Houses were made of adobe, sun-dried mud. Even the churches and the governor's Palace were mud. The buildings squatted square and brown on the ground. Nothing in Santa Fe was half so fine as a Comanche village of many tepees of buffalo hides. Comanche villages could be picked up and packed onto the backs of ponies. Comanches followed the buffalo herds.

Jacinto waited for an ox-drawn wagon to pass. Then, turning west, he started across the Plaza when suddenly he heard the tinkling of a bell, not one of the great church bells he loved but a small unpleasant-sounding handbell. He had to halt once more as a small procession came toward him, hurrying past the Governor's Palace. A bell man led it, followed by two boys in white surplices and an old priest in a long brown robe—Padre Luna in person. When Jacinto felt the old man's eyes on him, he knelt down and crossed himself. He knew that the priest was carrying the Sacred Heart to a dying man. He also knew he'd better kneel to show proper respect, or Don Hilario would hear that he had not and Jacinto would surely feel the anger of the *disciplina* again.

The twilight bell started to ring for Vespers just as Jacinto got up. This bell called for two minutes of silent prayer throughout all Santa Fe. Jacinto stood in the oncoming night, shivering in the cool wind. His head felt particularly cold. When he'd come to Santa Fe he had long braids and wore a buckskin shirt. His moccasins had beads and a piece of buffalo beard sewn on their back seams, and he wore jingling seashells in his pierced ears. All his Comanche finery was gone now, his hair cut, and his earrings crushed to powder by Don Hilario's order. They had tried to make a New Mexican of him, but they hadn't succeeded.

Jacinto didn't pray during Vespers. He thought of his father who was Big Wolf and of his always-laughing mother. Three years ago Big Wolf had taken his oldest son with him down into Mexico to trade buffalo robes for knives, hatchets, and cloth. The trading finished, Big Wolf started back to his village, camping on a Texas riverbank. There he had led a small raid against a horse herd belonging to a Mexican rancher. Against his father's orders Jacinto had trailed the Comanche men on his pony. Big Wolf and his braves had driven off the Mexican horses successfully, but some cowboys, turning back from chasing the fleet Comanches, had caught Jacinto trying to join his father.

Big Wolf did not come after his son. The boy knew why. His father had returned to his tribe to gather more warriors. But the Mexicans knew what he was doing too, and decided to get rid of the boy before the Comanches came again. The great fair at Santa Fe in the north was the place to sell him and also to make a profit to cover the loss of the horses. Jacinto had been taken to New Mexico and sold to Don Hilario Delacruz for a barrel of Taos-made whiskey. Other Indian children were sold as slaves at the fair that year of 1839, Jacinto learned later. There were Apache and Navajo children captured by the Pueblo Indians and even two

Comanche girls from another band. The girls had been
sold to a family in Taos. Jacinto had spoken with them
once and never seen them again.

He knew there was no hope of freedom for him, not
unless he stole Delacruz's chestnut stallion and rode
him out of Santa Fe. And someday soon he'd do just
that, Jacinto vowed as the bell for Vespers tolled to its
end. He had learned Spanish and the ways of the New
Mexicans, but he had not forgotten the Comanche language and the ways of his people. He would never
forget them! And he would never call himself Jacinto
Delacruz, taking his *patrón*'s last name as most Indian
captives did. "Jacinto," alone, was bad enough!

One wood seller remained at this late hour in Burro
Alley, his burro piled high with wood. The man knew
Jacinto from the many trips he'd made before. He
helped the boy load the Delacruz donkey hastily and
gave it a shove to start it moving.

Jacinto went back through the darkening town, not
hurrying though he knew he should. He enjoyed being
alone. He even dared to stand on tiptoe outside the
governor's Palace, hoping to see into the governor's
office where, he'd been told, the severed ears of Indians
who had rebelled against the Government had been
nailed to the wall. But he wasn't tall enough to see
inside. He could lean against a wall, though, and
listen to the guitar music coming from La Fonda.

The boy came at last to the blue front door of the

Delacruz house, which was surrounded by a high mud wall. He went to a side gate, barred at this time of night from the inside, and shouted to be let in.

Esperanza herself came, her black *rebozo* thrown over her head. "You've been gone half the night," she scolded. "Bring wood to the kitchen and the *patrón's* chamber. He wants to speak with you."

Jacinto untied the load with two jerks of the rope and let the wood clatter to the flagstones. This carelessness was too much for Esperanza, who was already angry. Her palm cracked across Jacinto's face. "*Ay de mí*. Don Hilario is reading, and you make as much noise as you can." Then she hurried across the courtyard into the house, shaking her head.

Burning with anger, Jacinto followed her, a load of wood in his arms. The kitchen was a large room with a clay-plastered floor, a fireplace, and a big table. From its beamed ceiling were suspended strings of onions, peas, and peppers. Copper pots hung on the wall next to a cabinet filled with silver plates—plates to be used only by the Delacruz family. Jacinto's nose told him supper was cooking, chili with beef for the servants and a savory stew for the family. Two cooks were at work, the old woman who'd served the Delacruz family for years, and the new cook, a young woman who made the morning chocolate and the fruit syrups Donato liked so well.

Jacinto dumped half of his wood at the side of the fire, then went out of the kitchen through the house. The thick white-washed walls set off the heavy dark tables, stools, and leather chests placed on the red-tile floors. Brass candlesticks were reflected in gold-framed mirrors. As Jacinto passed a birdcage, a green and scarlet parrot from Mexico cried out to him, "*Anda, anda.* (Move on, move on.)" Like everyone else in the house, the bird gave orders to him. He glowered at it, then went down three steps into a hallway. The house of Delacruz was old and large by Santa Fe standards. It had been added onto in many directions for years as Delacruz sons married and brought home their brides.

His arms full, the Comanche boy touched the door of his master's chamber with his foot.

"Enter," called Don Hilario's voice.

Coming into the man's bedchamber, Jacinto jerked his head at his *patrón*, but the motion was only a sham of a servant's bow. Don Hilario was sitting in a chair next to his huge canopied bed, reading. Donato sat on a stool staring into the fire, his slender back to the door. Jacinto stiffened. He hated the other boy.

Don Hilario put down his book and looked at Jacinto. He sighed, then said, "My housekeeper tells me that you do not obey her unless she shouts at you."

"She shouts all the time," said the boy, as he piled the wood next to the fire.

"Padre Luna says you pay no attention to what he tells you in confirmation classes and never cross yourself as you pass a church."

Jacinto was silent. This charge was true. He didn't want the religion of the New Mexicans. The faith of the Comanches was better. When a Comanche warrior died, he rode into the sun on his pony with his lance, bow, and shield. He lived for a time in the sun, then was born again of the Earth Mother as a Comanche. Who could want more than that?

"But that is not all," complained Don Hilario. "Donato has something to say to you."

Donato arose. Tall and elegant in flaring velvet trousers trimmed with silver buttons down the side, he towered over Jacinto. Donato held out his hand. In it lay a woman's enameled bracelet, set with black pearls and coral. "This was our dead mother's. Have you ever seen it before?"

"No, *patrón*, I have not." The glitter in Donato's eyes made Jacinto wary.

"My sister wears it sometimes. When she discovered it was missing, we searched the house. It was found under your pile of hides tonight."

Fury rose in Jacinto's chest. No, he'd never seen the bracelet, but he'd seen the silver coins Donato had left in plain sight in his own bedchamber to tempt Jacinto as he cleaned it. Scenting the trap set for him, Jacinto had cleaned very carefully around the money, not touching it. Donato had wanted to see him whipped again. Donato wanted this whipping so badly that he himself had put the bracelet under Jacinto's pile of deerskins used for a bed. Donato liked to watch the servants whipped. At these times there was a devil in him. Even Esperanza said she could see it in Donato's eyes. Jacinto and the other servants knew that a worried Don Hilario had spoken once with Padre Luna about Donato's cruelty.

Now Donato yelled, "You stole the bracelet!"

"No." Jacinto folded his arms across his chest.

The other boy put the bracelet down on a table. He raised his hand as Esperanza had and struck Jacinto across the mouth. This time Jacinto couldn't control his anger as he had with the woman. He hit Donato with his clenched hand as hard as he could and knocked him onto the hard tiles.

"Jacinto!" cried Don Hilario, as the Indian boy stooped and swiftly picked up the fireplace poker. The man was on him at once, grabbing the poker away and flinging Jacinto against the wall. "Esteban! Porfirio!" he shouted, standing guard over his son, holding Jacinto at bay with the poker.

Sandaled feet came running down the hallway. In a moment two Indian menservants were in the room. Jacinto saw how their eyes flicked anxiously from Donato to Don Hilario to Jacinto. The men, both Navajos also captured as children, were wary.

"Esteban, find Padre Luna," Don Hilario ordered the older of the Navajos.

"Get the *alcalde,* too, Father," whined Donato, who was getting up.

Jacinto moved closer to the door. The *alcalde* was the mayor of Santa Fe. If he came he would bring the city guards with him, and that would mean jail or maybe worse. Indians were not to strike *patróns.* Jacinto kept his eyes on Don Hilario. Surely he knew Donato had been lying.

Delacruz spoke again to Esteban. "Ask Padre Luna to bring the man Gamboa with him if Gamboa is still in Santa Fe. I have need of him."

"*Sí, patrón.*" The Navajo hurried out of the room.

"You did not tell him to get the *alcalde,*" Donato complained.

"We shall not need him. This is not a matter for all of Santa Fe to discuss. Go to your bedchamber, Donato, and remain there until I call for you. On the way take the bracelet to your sister."

Donato pointed to Jacinto. "What of him?"

"The Indian will be dealt with." Delacruz spoke to the younger Navajo, a powerfully built man who used the whip on the servants. "Take Jacinto to my study and guard him well."

"I did not steal the bracelet, *patrón,*" said Jacinto, as Donato passed him, glaring.

Don Hilario shook his head. "No, I suspect you more

than likely did not. But Donato is my son. And I think you would have killed him just now. This cannot be forgotten."

Jacinto looked at his feet. Where Esperanza's blow had angered him, Donato's had maddened him. Yes, he might have killed Donato. With the Navajo gripping him by the shoulder, Jacinto was led to the small dim room where Delacruz often conducted business.

"Who is Gamboa?" Jacinto asked the Navajo.

The man shook his head. "I do not know. I have not heard the name."

They waited in silence for a time, and then the other Navajo returned, breathing hard from running. Behind him came Padre Luna, his skirts hiked up for speed, and a stranger, a short, broad man with bright dark eyes. He wore a serape of striped black and gray wool, Pueblo-type leather boots, and leather trousers. In one hand he held his broad-brimmed black hat. By his humble dress, the stranger was not a *caballero*. Jacinto looked into his face and in spite of himself jerked with recognition. The man was an Indian, which was not at all unusual in Santa Fe. But unless Jacinto missed his guess, he was also a Comanche.

Don Hilario came into the room soon after Esteban went to get him. Delacruz greeted the padre and the stranger with his usual great politeness, then asked the stranger, "You are Santos Gamboa of Abiquiu, Padre Luna's friend?"

"*Sí, patrón,* I am."

"And you will leave Santa Fe tomorrow?"

Padre Luna spoke for Gamboa. "As soon as he and his people hear Mass in the morning."

"Excellent." Delacruz gestured toward Jacinto. "This boy speaks Spanish. He has been of my household for three years. Will you take him with you, Gamboa? I give him to you."

"What has he done that you want to have me take him?" Gamboa was frowning. "Is he a thief?"

"No." Don Hilario's reply was quick and to Jacinto's way of thinking fair. "He is not at all suited for the life of a house servant."

Gamboa nodded. "I will take him."

"I'll give you twenty reales. They will buy many bullets for your muskets."

Padre Luna laughed. "Save your reales, Don Hilario. You do not know Santos. He will take no gifts from you. Equip Jacinto for a journey. That will be enough. See that he has strong boots and give him a burro or donkey."

"Where do I go?" Jacinto asked Padre Luna, his gaze still fixed on Santos Gamboa. Yes, he was more and more sure that he was a Comanche. Was Gamboa traveling east to the plains to trade with the Comanches? The New Mexicans were clever. They would send a Comanche they could trust to the Comanches.

"You go to the Rancho San Bernardino," said Padre

Luna. Then he added, "You will not return to Santa Fe, Jacinto. Santos is taking a party of settlers there."

"Rancho San Bernardino is in California," Don Hilario said, looking away from Jacinto.

California! The word was little more than a name to Jacinto. He'd never talked with anyone who'd been to California and knew only that it was a great distance from Santa Fe and in the *wrong* direction for a Comanche—to the west.

Jacinto stared into Gamboa's eyes and spoke in the Comanche language. "I am named Spotted Wild Horse. Do you understand what I'm saying?"

Santos Gamboa nodded. Jacinto felt like smiling but he didn't. His new *patrón* was indeed a Comanche.

THE ROUTE FROM SANTA FE
TO RANCHO SAN BERNARDINO

Places within brackets were named
after the period in which the story takes place.

0   50   100
Scale of Miles

UTAH

[Parowan]

NEVADA

JOURNEY OF DEATH

[Las Vegas]

Resting Spring

CALIFORNIA

MOJAVE DESERT

[Barstow]

Mojave River

Cajon Pass

San Bernardino Mountains

San Gabriel
Mission

GRAND CANYON

Los Angeles

Santa Ana R.

Rancho San Bernardino

Colorado River

ARIZONA

Pacific
Ocean

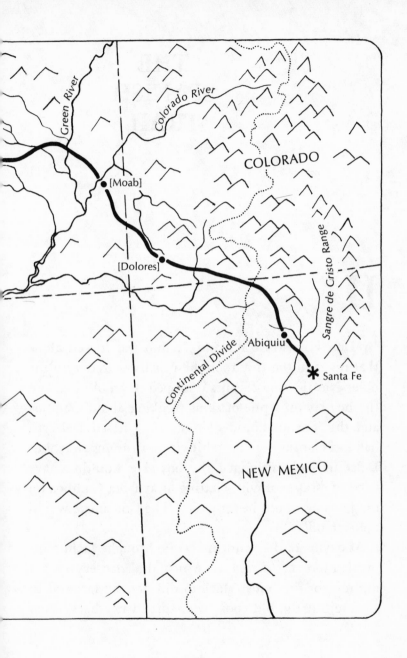

THE
SPANISH
TRAIL

II

By Don Hilario's command Jacinto was locked alone
that night in the tiny room he usually shared with the
older Navajo manservant. Wrapped in an old blanket,
the boy lay on a pile of skins thinking about Gamboa
and the journey ahead of him. He guessed Delacruz
had locked him in to keep him from running away, but
Delacruz had misjudged the boy. He wouldn't have
tried to escape tonight. Getting away from Gamboa on
the journey would be far easier. The Comanche would
understand.

At daybreak the younger Navajo brought Jacinto his
breakfast of *tortillas* after which the manservant led
him out of the house. Jacinto did not say farewell to
anyone but the old cook, who turned her back when

he passed. The older Navajo waited beside the gate, holding the halter of the donkey Jacinto had loaded with wood the day before. Now it carried a pack, containing the supplies Don Hilario was giving the boy.

With the two Navajo menservants alongside him, Jacinto went quickly and happily through Santa Fe to the Plaza. He'd make his escape when the caravan was on its way. It was assembling now in front of the Palace of the Governors. Jacinto saw laden mules, men in boots, children and women with *rebozos* over their heads. The many dogs of Santa Fe were barking and nipping at the heels of the mules and being kicked at for their boldness. Padre Luna stood talking with Santos Gamboa and three other men, but when he spied Jacinto and the two Navajos the priest came over to them.

"You did not hear Mass this morning with the others, Jacinto," Padre Luna accused.

The older Navajo explained, "Don Hilario did not order us to bring him to church."

Padre Luna frowned. "What supplies does he have?"

"What Gamboa told our *patrón* the settlers should have, Padre. Biscuit, dried meat in buckskin sacks, beans, and cornmeal. The boy has blankets and clothing."

The priest smiled. "Then all Jacinto requires is a blessing. Kneel down."

Jacinto knelt in the dust to permit the priest to put

his hands on his head and say a prayer over him. He thought of telling him that Donato had lied, but decided against it.

Why irritate the old priest now? Hearing later that he'd run away from the caravan would be annoyance enough for him. Jacinto would send Padre Luna a message somehow and another to Don Hilario and Donato.

After Jacinto arose, one of the men who'd been conferring with Santos Gamboa came over to him. He was a young man who strongly resembled Gamboa. Jacinto guessed he might be his son. Jacinto spoke to him in Comanche as the young man took Jacinto's donkey from the Navajo who had been leading it.

"I am Hipolito Gamboa," the young man said in Spanish to Jacinto. "Our father now has the license we needed from the governor. We are ready to go. Come with me."

Jacinto left the two Navajo servants and the priest quickly and without a backward glance. He'd never see them again. He'd never return to Santa Fe—Don Hilario had been correct about that.

The caravan was nearly ready. Hipolito Gamboa put Jacinto's donkey into line between two mules bearing double packs. A young woman in a purple skirt was stationed behind the first mule. She had a stick in her hand but a smile for Jacinto, who guessed she was a Pueblo Indian by the high white boots she wore. "I am wife to Hipolito Gamboa," she told him.

Uninterested in her, Jacinto looked to the head of the caravan and saw that Santos Gamboa was leading a white mare along by her halter. The bell around the mare's neck clanged in the cold morning air, a sign to the mules and the people that they were on their way. When it came time for his donkey to start walking, too, Jacinto called out, *"Anda, mula,"* and struck its flank with his palm. The settlers Gamboa was leading to California either took off their hats or dropped clumsy curtseys to Padre Luna as they passed, but not Jacinto. He kept his eyes fixed on the pack on his donkey's back, calculating how far the supplies in it would take him when he escaped. He'd check the store of food as soon as possible. Perhaps he'd steal the white mare when he left. It would be only an instant's work with a knife to cut the bell from around her neck. And then he would be free!

Santos Gamboa took the caravan northwards on the Spanish Trail out of Santa Fe toward the sharp-peaked Sangre de Cristo Mountains. Jacinto looked back only once at the town of mud he had despised, grinned, and stared ahead at the green meadows dotted with small round bushes of a darker green. The day was crisp and sunny. The sky was a very deep blue strewn with white clouds that looked like small puffs of smoke from a Comanche pipe. Cottonwoods and aspens shone golden in the clear bright light of early autumn.

Gamboa made camp that first night at an Indian

village some miles from Santa Fe. Here Jacinto learned
that to escape would not be so easy as he thought. Hipolito Gamboa was beside him the moment they stopped,
helping him unpack the donkey. While Jacinto looked
through his supplies, the young man stood over him,
examining them, too. Suddenly he reached down into
the pile of goods and plucked out the knife Don Hilario
had provided.

Hipolito said, "You will eat at my campfire and sleep
near it. My wife will cook for you. You will have no
need of this knife."

Jacinto flared up. "Your father told you to take my
knife!"

Hipolito nodded. "*Sí*, he did. He promised Padre
Luna this morning that you would go to California
with us and not run off to Comanche lands. Without
a weapon you will have to come with us. You will be
guarded well by me and others."

"You think I was going to run away?" Jacinto looked
longingly at the knife Hipolito put into the sash around
his waist.

Young Gamboa laughed. "*Sí*, our father says it is
what he would have done when he was your age."

"Then why doesn't he let me go now?"

"Because he gave his word to the priest and your
patrón that you would go to California. He wants to
make certain that you do not steal the bell mare or a

mule and run away from us. Without a knife and with
a donkey so old, you would be wise not to try."

Jacinto exploded. "Santos Gamboa is no Comanche
now!"

Hipolito laughed. "It is true. He does not follow
Comanche ways, though he says he remembers them.
He is a Genizaro. Our mother is a Pueblo."

Jacinto shook his head. Genizaros were captives from
many Indian tribes who'd become New Mexicans and
Christians. He would not be a Genizaro! "Then if you
are happy here in New Mexico, why do you go to California?" he asked Hipolito.

"For the land. There is much land there and much
water." Hipolito left Jacinto and went over to the
campfire of his father and unmarried brothers. Jacinto
leaned against his donkey, scowling, aware that many
eyes besides Hipolito's were on him. Clearly Santos
Gamboa had warned people in the caravan that the
Comanche boy was to be watched or he would try to
escape.

Two days later the Gamboas, who purchased fifty
sheep near the tiny town of Abiquiu, gave Jacinto a
task. He was set to sheepherding. Jacinto despised the
foolish sheep, but he followed after them, shouting
often at them as he guided the flock with a stout stick.
Although he walked at the end of the caravan, probably
the best place of all to escape from, he couldn't fall

back and disappear into the yellow aspens. Three others were always with him, two boys younger than himself and one or the other of the Gamboa sons, all taller and stronger than Jacinto.

The New Mexicans made slow progress. By the time they had been on the Trail a week, they had come only a hundred miles from Santa Fe. Each night Gamboa tried to halt at a place that had water and grass for the mules and sheep. Plains-born Jacinto disliked the tree-covered mountains. The Trail ascended so steeply at times that he was forced to toil up it and in other places to slide down, taking care not to fall among the sheep, scattering them. The Spanish Trail was little more than a track through wild country. No wagon or oxcart could travel it in the mountains, and when it wound along the edge of a gully, Jacinto and the other shepherds had to work hard to keep the sheep in single file. If the animals tumbled over the edge, Hipolito Gamboa warned, they would pile on top of one another and suffocate.

Weary every night, Jacinto shivered in his blankets as he listened to the shrieks of pumas prowling the camp on the scent of mule flesh. At these times he was glad of the settlers' muskets, though he wished still that he had his knife.

Santos Gamboa, Jacinto noted, used rivers as location points. Sometimes his caravan followed them for days at a stretch and finally splashed across at a shallow ford.

Wading into the cold water relieved Jacinto's feet, which often burned. He'd noticed, too, that the back of his donkey, being urged along by Hipolito's wife with her own mule, was getting sore from its packsaddle. The journey was telling on the animals and the people. Gamboa's New Mexicans were becoming more quiet each night as they made camp. They knew that many, many hard miles were ahead of them. And as yet they had known no real hardship.

Hipolito talked one night with some settlers at his campfire while Jacinto sat against a rock, his blanket around him. Tonight, although his feet ached, Jacinto felt almost at ease. The previous day they'd camped by another river, one so filled with fish that the men could wade in and pull them out of shallow water. Jacinto had proven his Comanche spirit by refusing to eat the fish. Comanches never ate fish, but he'd noticed that Santos Gamboa did.

Hipolito was answering questions from other settlers. "Sí, from Santa Fe to the pueblo of Los Angeles requires two months of travel."

"But will the Mexican rancheros truly give us land in California?" a man from Taos asked.

"It is promised—land for each man, land on the banks of a river. My father has seen the land and the river," replied Hipolito.

An older New Mexican demanded suspiciously, "Why will Mexicans in California give anything to us?

Mexicans give Indians little and take much, it seems to me, in Santa Fe. All Indians know that Mexicans can change themselves into owls at dark. We are Indians."

Young Gamboa sounded disgusted. "You have been told the answer to this by my father. We have muskets and can use them well. We shall protect the California rancheros from Indian raiders."

The older man had a handful of piñon nuts. He cracked one, ate it, then said, "It is a strange thing, I think, to hire Indians to fight Indians."

Hipolito replied, "It is the way things are done in California. The Mexican rancheros are bedeviled by Indians who come down and drive off their herds."

"They have many cows?" asked the first settler.

"Many, many cows, but it is not cows the Indians seek."

"What is it then? Sheep?"

"No." Hipolito made a broad gesture over the fire. "It is horses they want. Our father says the plains of California are covered with herds of horses, the finest in all the world. He has seen them."

Horses! Jacinto sat up straight, hoping to hear more about horses. No one had told him that California was horse country, though Don Hilario had once said something about buying a big California mule someday.

The old man spoke again. "What Indians are we to fight? Apaches or Navajos?"

Young Gamboa laughed. "Not unless we must fight

them on our way to California. We travel far to the north to avoid the great canyon of the River Colorado and the hunting grounds of the Apaches and Navajos. Where we shall go it is the Utes who raid for horses. They raid Rancho San Bernardino."

Utes! Jacinto almost joined the men at the fire. Comanches and Utes were enemies. His father often had boasted that he had killed two Ute warriors in battle.

The old man asked the question that was burning Jacinto. "Will the rancheros give us many horses, too?"

Hipolito shook his head. "We shall have little need of horses. The oxen we can buy will be enough for farmers. The mules of this caravan are not ours. They shall be returned to Don Quirino Aldama, the ranchero who loaned them to our father to bring us from New Mexico."

Jacinto smiled in the shadows. So, he was the only one who truly owned an animal, even if it was only a donkey. He pulled his hat down over his eyes and his blanket closer as he thought over his situation. He had been traveling for two weeks and had no idea how far they were from Santa Fe. Although he could escape and follow the tracks the caravan had made, there were pumas around almost every night, and the remarks Hipolito made about Apaches and Navajos weren't exactly comforting. On the other hand, the prospect of seeing many, many horses and fighting Utes was very tempting. Yes, Spotted Wild Horse, son of Big Wolf, would travel all the way to California. As for Gamboa's settlers not having horses, Spotted Wild Horse, the Comanche, intended to have one. And he would never farm. Comanches rode proudly over the land. They didn't work it with a spade or a plow.

The boy dreamed. What would Big Wolf say if his son returned one day with a string of fine California horses? Yes, he might do just that. He'd keep his eyes open and mark the rivers and mountains of the Spanish Trail well in his memory so he could travel it again someday.

The next morning Jacinto went up to Santos Gamboa and said in the Comanche tongue, "I will give you my promise that I will not run away."

Gamboa, who was cinching the packsaddle on a mule, grunted with effort, then asked, "Why do you say that now?" He spoke in Spanish.

Although the man's insistence on speaking Spanish annoyed Jacinto, he used the language, too. "I want to go to California to see the many horses. Give my knife back to me, and I will help you fight our Comanche enemies, the Utes."

Gamboa looked hard at the boy for a long moment. "I accept your word. Tell Hipolito to return the knife to you. No one shall watch you from now on." He added, "Padre Luna told me before we left Santa Fe that your *patrón* said his son accused you of stealing."

"I did not steal, *patrón*."

The man smiled. "Have you thought, Jacinto, that you are a slave no longer? Do not call me *patrón*. Delacruz gave you to me, but I will not accept you." Gamboa turned away to speak to his overweight wife, who would drive the mule.

Jacinto walked away, pondering the remark. So Santos Gamboa did not consider himself his master. The thought was pleasant. Clearly Gamboa understood him. He would not care if he left as soon as he'd seen the California horses and perhaps fought a Ute. Jacinto decided that he respected this man in spite of the fact that he was a Genizaro, not a Comanche any longer. Gamboa had given him his freedom. Jacinto hadn't had to steal it by running away.

In the weeks that followed, Jacinto began to learn what Gamboa had meant about the hardness of the journey. The way through the mountains was difficult, chill, and wet. The people of the caravan shuddered with cold under trees that dripped rain on them all night long. Though it was not even the first of October, they had to move through hard-packed snow in some of the highest places. Many mornings they went without breakfast to get an early start because the skies were threatening. At other times they camped early where they could find grass for the animals but where there was no water, except for what they carried with them. One river they came to was wide and rapid.

Jacinto helped the men build rafts from river trees and stood watching as women and children were ferried across by men with long poles. Jacinto, who couldn't swim, crossed by holding onto the halter of a swimming mule. Only half the number of sheep were left now; the others had been killed along the Trail for food or had died. Those that remained were ferried across, bleating, by Gamboa and his sons, who made trip after trip over the river.

The country beyond this river dismayed many of the settlers. Here the land was barren, without grass for the mules. Women and children had to slice bark from cottonwood trees to feed them. Jacinto hand-fed leaves to his sore-backed donkey every night they camped.

Three days farther on they found both water and grass, and Gamboa called a day's halt, so the mules and sheep could graze. The next day they stopped again, this time because of rain and a violent hailstorm that drove everyone to hunt for shelter. Even so, hailstones the size of hens' eggs bruised Jacinto's shoulders.

A new trouble began to plague the New Mexicans during the next stage of the journey to California. Grass was high in the mountain meadows and the water the settlers came across was pure and cold. But no wood was to be found anywhere. They used sagebrush for the campfires, though it made poor fuel in the estimation of the women. Now, while he gathered brush for

Hipolito's wife, for the first time Jacinto thought with longing of Burro Alley in Sante Fe.

That same night Santos Gamboa went from fire to fire to tell the settlers they must start carrying wood as well as water. Jacinto was rubbing grease into the sores on his donkey's back as he listened to the man. If it wasn't lack of grass, it was lack of water, and if not water, wood. *Sí*, the journey was very hard. Men and animals were growing thin. Jacinto could count the ribs of his donkey.

But Gamboa led them on, and soon they were descending from the highlands. Jacinto kept a tally of scratches on the stick he used to drive the sheep. They were forty days away from Santa Fe, but according to Gamboa still very far from Rancho San Bernardino.

In the valley of a river so muddy it looked like chocolate, the New Mexicans encountered their first band of Indians. They were afoot. Guarding his donkey, Jacinto kept his hand on his knife while Santos Gamboa spoke in Spanish with the leader of the Indians, who were short and dark-skinned.

"What do they want?" he heard Teresa Gamboa ask her husband, Hipolito. "Are they Utes?"

Santos Gamboa, hearing his daughter-in-law, turned around. "No, they are Piutes, a harmless people. I know them from my last journey. They will sell us green corn and beans if we will give them two sheep."

Hipolito Gamboa's fire that night was graced by two
Piutes, who shared their beans and cornmeal and upset
Hipolito's wife by roasting lizards over the fire on sticks
and eating them. Jacinto watched the almost naked
Piutes with disgust. They were a spiritless people, not
half the equal of Comanches. They had no muskets and
few belongings, except for baskets and rabbit-skin
robes. They weren't worthy enemies.

The caravan left the valley at dawn the next morning, hoping to make as much progress as possible over
what Santos Gamboa warned everyone personally was
one of the worst parts of the Spanish Trail, the *jornada
del muerto* (journey of death) near sixty Yankee miles
of high country without water or grass. With the others,
Jacinto soon learned why this part of the Trail had
earned such an ominous name. It was nothing but great
distances of yellow sand and spiny plants and sun-
bleached skeletons of mules and horses. His feet swelled
so in his boots that he couldn't get them off at night.
Like everyone else, he looked for the barrel cactus, but
the plant was rare and no New Mexican spied one.
Jacinto had no water at all the last day in this horrible
country but one mouthful to wash down some parched
corn. His donkey fared better on the dried grass he'd
added to the animal's load.

At the end of the *jornada del muerto* lay the wondrous meadow, Las Vegas, where there was not only

grass but hot springs. Las Vegas was also occupied by a band of Piutes, but they fled from the oncoming caravan, and Jacinto was not sorry to see them run away. After resting there they went up into the mountains once more, traveling over gravel and sharp rocks that could harm the hooves of the mules. Two of them, weakened by the *jornada del muerto*, fell on the Trail and had to be shot. Their packs were unloaded and distributed among the other animals.

At a place Gamboa called Resting Spring the caravan halted for three days of rest and preparation. Water was stored in every receptacle they had. Grass was pulled and piled onto the top of each mule's load. They were to travel over their second desert, the Mojave. But they would not journey by day. Midafternoon of the fourth day the man led out the white bell mare while Jacinto waited beside the Trail with the remaining ten sheep. Each morning Gamboa and the settlers had prayed on their knees for the blessing of God on their journey. This afternoon prayer had been the longest yet, longer even than the one they'd said when they faced the *jornada del muerto*.

There was nothing in the Mojave but rough sand and wind, cruel, prickly plants, flinty rocks, and the beds of bone-dry lakes. Jacinto's feet blistered and bled. The caravan traveled southwest, using the North Star at its back for a guide. A gale of wind enveloped them as they halted at a place where bitter water could be found. Jacinto was so weary that he scarcely heard Santos Gamboa announcing to the settlers that they were in California and near the end of their journey.

The next evening they started out again over the seemingly endless desert. Everyone stumbled along in silence. Not even the babies or young children cried in the black night. The only sounds Jacinto heard were the tinkling of the bell mare's bell, the creaking of packsaddles, and the whine of the hot wind. The boy had bound his feet in rags inside his rock-torn boots and put rawhide shoes on his donkey's hooves, but these precautions did little good. The donkey limped badly. And there were only six sheep left. The others had lain down and died beside the Trail, leaving their bones with the bones of other animals.

Suddenly near dawn of the third day over this terrible desert, Jacinto's tiny flock started to bleat wildly and the mules to bray. The sheep began to run. Jacinto lurched after them, knowing they had scented water, which turned out to be Mojave River, a shallow, broad stream bordered with green cottonwoods. The animals lumbered into the river to drink. As for Jacinto, he and the smaller boys waded out into it and flopped down to let the water run over their bodies. From his place in the river, Jacinto watched Santos Gamboa kneel again and lead his people in thanksgiving for the safe passage over this second desert.

The grass was poor beside the river but there would
be very fine grazing soon, Gamboa announced as
they made camp. They were nearing Rancho San
Bernardino at last. When Jacinto took the packsaddle
off his donkey that morning, the animal wandered off
to find grass. Jacinto hadn't bothered to hobble him
so he wouldn't stray; the donkey wasn't strong enough
to go far. Actually he was weaker than Jacinto had
guessed. When the boy went to look for him at dusk,
he found the animal lying beside the river, dead. Two
coyotes sat not far from the body, eyeing the boy
warily but too bold and hungry to move away.

Jacinto didn't mourn the donkey. He lifted its head
and removed the halter, then left the carcass to the
coyotes. After all, the donkey had come from Don
Hilario Delacruz, a man who had made a slave of him.
What were donkeys anyhow compared to horses?

That evening Jacinto sat by Hipolito's campfire
gazing at the blue-black outline of the San Bernardino
Mountains. The surviving mules of the caravan would
take the goods his donkey had carried to California for
him. What he owned he would reclaim later. Santos
Gamboa had declared that these mountains were the
last the settlers would have to climb. They must go
through a stretch of hilly country called Cajon Pass,
which they would descend into the beautiful land
that held Rancho San Bernardino. The Land of Many
Horses, Jacinto called it in his mind.

THE
LAND
OF
MANY
HORSES

III

Jacinto had debated with himself asking the New Mexicans to call him Spotted Wild Horse, now that he was no one's slave. But he decided that it made little difference to him what they called him. Santos Gamboa would speak only Spanish to him. There were other Comanches in the caravan, Jacinto had learned from one of the boy shepherds, but they, too, spoke Spanish even to one another, which marked them for certain as Genizaros like Gamboa. He'd stay in California only long enough to scout some very good horses for stealing and to fight some Utes. Yes, he thought, he could travel back over the Spanish Trail with his horses and bypass Santa Fe, even though it would be very dangerous alone.

Not one of Gamboa's weary settlers shouted with
happiness as they gathered at the end of high Cajon
Pass to take their first look at the plain where they
would live the rest of their lives. Jacinto watched them
cross themselves and kneel while Gamboa gave thanks
for their accomplished journey. They'd lost nineteen
mules, most of the sheep, and Jacinto's donkey. One
elderly man and one small girl had died on the *jornada
del muerto*. It had been a God-favored trip in spite
of these losses. The man's widow should be given the
land due her husband, and the loss of the child was
to be expected for she had been sickly to begin with.
Gamboa had warned her parents to leave her in New
Mexico with relatives, but they had refused.

While the settlers prayed, Jacinto stood, his arms
folded, looking down at his destination. From this far
away he could make out nothing but yellow-brown
grassland broken here and there by masses of green
and groups of rocks and jutting hills. A heavy line of
green followed a wandering pattern, probably trees
bordering the river that Hipolito Gamboa had talked
about. In one spot Jacinto thought he could even spy
a thread of blue water. Facing west, he saw a haze of
yellow dust in the distance. His heart suddenly beat
faster. A herd of moving horses made such a cloud, but
so did moving cattle. His Land of Many Horses was
blocked off by mountains on two sides but lay open to
the west and south. And it was enormous. Jacinto had

heard Santos Gamboa say once that the California grazing lands stretched from the mountains to the sea. Gamboa himself had seen the ocean on a trading expedition to the pueblo of Los Angeles. The sea was amazingly broad and had remarkable colors that kept changing, and it made much noise. Yes, Jacinto should see this ocean of Gamboa's, too, just to be able to tell the Honey-Eater Comanches when he rejoined them that he'd looked upon its wonder.

Santos Gamboa got up at last and put on his hat. He spoke to his people, "There is no church and there is no priest where we go."

"We will build a church, and we will get a priest somehow," said the newly widowed Carmela Gomez.

Jacinto grunted. Build a church? Not Spotted Wild Horse!

Gamboa spoke to the woman courteously. "*Sí*, but first we must build homes." He went to the bell mare, took her by the halter, and began to lead her down out of the mountains.

Jacinto waited until the caravan had gone by and the few remaining sheep had been driven past him by the other boy shepherds. Then he fell in behind them last of all. He was pleased to get out of the mountains where the air was hard to breathe and rocks cut into his torn boots. When he returned, he would ride a horse, as befit a Comanche man.

A north wind started blowing as they came out onto

the plain. It was laden with stinging bits of dust that got into his eyes and throat and made him cough. In spite of the autumn season the wind was uncomfortably hot. When they halted to rest, Jacinto heard Gamboa call it the "devil wind."

During their halt the boy watched several New Mexicans stoop and pick up a handful of the yellow-brown earth. They looked closely at it, crumbled it between their fingers, and let the wind blow it away. Two men discussed the soil.

"It is good land even if I have seen swamps and some very dry places today," one said.

The second man agreed. "The soil is very rich. I think it will grow much corn and beans."

Jacinto, who had been squatting near them resting, saw the two settlers move closer together. The first man asked, "What of this Don Quirino Aldama that Gamboa speaks of? Will he be a kind of *patrón*?"

"He will not own us," said the second man. "We are our own masters here in California."

The other New Mexican shook his head. "Santos Gamboa put his name to a piece of paper Don Quirino gave him."

The second man, a farmer from Taos, laughed. "That does not make us slaves, Francisco. The Mexican governor in Santa Fe would not permit such a thing."

"The governor of New Mexico is not also the governor of California. These Mexican rancheros here in California must be very powerful to have so much land they can give it away to us just to protect their herds from Indians who sometimes raid. This Don Quirino could think of himself as our *patrón*!"

"Santos Gamboa will see that this does not happen."

"The mules are Don Quirino's," Francisco said. "We cannot go back to New Mexico without them. We cannot steal them from him or take California horses."

"No." The farmer was somber. "I have heard how Californios treat a man who steals a horse from them. They do not hang him from a tree. They throw a *reata* around him and gallop away, dragging him to his death over the ground. It is said they love their horses more than their wives and children. One who dares to steal a horse from them must be very stupid."

"Or very bold and clever, like a Comanche," Jacinto muttered to himself. A Comanche man would steal a horse from under its rider. That's what Yankees were supposed to say about Comanches. Jacinto wondered if there were any Yankees in California, too. He'd seen them trading in Santa Fe—big, blue-eyed, sometimes yellow-haired men. But he'd never spoken to an American and no American had ever spoken to him.

Santos Gamboa didn't go himself or send Hipolito to the ranch of Don Quirino Aldama. He led an advance party of New Mexicans in the middle of the afternoon to the banks of the river Jacinto had seen from the pass and let their mules drink in the shallow water. Hipolito asked Jacinto to accompany him to the river. Hipolito seemed to like Jacinto, who sometimes got the uncomfortable feeling that he amused Hipolito and his wife.

"Does your father say this is to be your land?" Jacinto asked the young man.

"I do not know," Hipolito answered.

"When will you get your land?"

"When Aldama comes."

"And when will that be?"

Hipolito pointed to his father, who had walked out from under the trees bordering the river onto the grass. Santos Gamboa, holding a musket in one hand fired it directly overhead, sending many birds flapping out of the sycamores and cottonwoods.

"Why does he do that?" asked Jacinto.

"To signal that we have come."

"And who will come?"

"A *vaquero* of Aldama's, probably. A cowboy should hear the shot."

"To own all this land Don Quirino must be a very great *patrón*. Will he come himself?"

"I do not know. I have never seen him." Then Hipolito asked, "What do you think of California?"

"It is good land for horses."

"It is good for many things. But my father says there are dangers here that no man sees because it seems so peaceful. There are rattlesnakes and also many bears—

great bears the Yankees call 'grizzlies,' as well as smaller bears."

"And Utes?" Jacinto put in hopefully.

"And Utes at times." Hipolito didn't seem as pleased as Jacinto at the thought of the raiders.

It seemed a long time before Gamboa's shot attracted anyone to the New Mexicans. But at last Jacinto, who'd climbed a sycamore to look over the plain, spied a rider coming from the east. He rode so swiftly that by the time Jacinto was down out of the tree, the man was in the camp, putting away his pistol and talking from horseback with Santos Gamboa. Jacinto's first thought was envious. What a handsome horse the Californian rode, golden with a darker golden mane and tail. It must be worth a great deal of money.

But as handsome as the horse was and as rich as its saddle and bridle were with silver, the rider outshone all. The spurs on his black boots were of silver with long star-shaped rowels. His big black hat was studded with silver sun-and-moon patterns. His trousers were dark blue velvet, slit up the the sides to show the pleated white linen pantaloons underneath. His jacket was light blue velvet and the blanket over his shoulder scarlet as blood. In the sash around his waist he had a knife in a silver sheath and a pearl-handled pistol. The Californian's face was as dazzling as his costume. He was young, only about five years older than Jacinto, and remarkably good-looking, far more handsome than Donato Delacruz. Touched by the sun, his skin had a bronze look to it. Under his hat he wore a red scarf tied to one side so his shoulder-length black curling hair showed.

Jacinto heard only his last words as the youth finished talking with Santos Gamboa. "*Sí,* I shall tell him." He turned his horse, touched him with a spur, and left the camp at a run.

Gamboa called to the men of his advance party, "Don Quirino Aldama is well and will come to us in the morning."

"Who was the young *vaquero?*" asked a settler, who seemed to have been as dazzled by the youth's splendor as Jacinto was.

"No *vaquero.* That was El Chino, Aldama's youngest son. I have seen him before."

"El Chino?" asked Hipolito.

"*Sí, chino*—man with the curly hair. All California *vaqueros* are not such dandies." Gamboa sounded disgusted.

"He rides as the devil rides," remarked Hipolito.

"Some men say El Chino is a devil," Gamboa said dryly. "But many Californians ride as he does."

"He must own many horses to ride one so hard," Jacinto put in.

"So many he does not know how many there are!"

Santos Gamboa shrugged and walked away to order men to go back and bring the other settlers to the camping place.

Halfway through the next morning Jacinto heard the sound of many horses coming. He put down the cow horn filled with grease he was using to doctor sores on a mule's back and came as close as he could to Santos Gamboa.

Seven men rode to the fires the women were just putting out, five Indian-looking *vaqueros* dressed in leather jackets and trousers, a red-faced man with a brown beard, and a thin, clean-shaven, middle-aged Mexican wearing a brown hat trimmed with gold braid. The Mexican's horse was the finest, a great black stallion that stood absolutely motionless when he was reined in. Jacinto knew he must be Aldama, in spite of his plain garments. Gamboa had taken off his hat for him where he had not for El Chino.

Everyone heard Aldama's voice. "I am pleased that you have had a safe journey, Gamboa. My agent, Señor Ross, will give you your land."

Santos Gamboa asked, "What of the Utes? Have they come recently?"

"*Sí*, they came at the time of the full moon two months ago. We think they were led by Walkara himself. One of my *vaqueros* saw the chief's face."

The brown-bearded man brought his horse forward close enough for Jacinto to see that the rider had light blue eyes. Don Quirino's agent was a Yankee who spoke good Spanish. "I hope you will have time, Gamboa, to build your homes before the Utes come again."

The leader of the New Mexicans replied, "We shall work as swiftly as we can."

Aldama nodded gravely. "I'll send Indians from my rancho to help you build huts."

Gamboa smiled. "It will not be necessary, Don Quirino."

The Yankee agent dismounted. He looked around for a moment, then gave the reins of his horse to Jacinto who took them proudly. Ross reached into a saddlebag and took out paper, a bottle of ink, and a quill. He went to a fallen log, sat down, uncorked the ink bottle, arranged the paper on his knee, and ordered, "Gamboa, I want the names of all your New Mexicans. I'll write yours first—Santos Gamboa of Abiquiu."

Jacinto held the American's horse while Gamboa led first his wife, then his sons, and then his oldest son's wife to the Yankee, who took down their names. Then Gamboa brought the others forward one by one while Aldama and his cowboys looked on from horseback. Finally only Carmela Gomez and Jacinto remained.

Gamboa gave the agent the woman's name, adding, "Her husband died on the Trail. I ask that she be given the land due to him."

Ross looked up sharply. "Who will work it for her?"

"All of the men here will help her, *señor*." Suddenly Gamboa swung about and looked at Jacinto. "The boy holding your horse will live in her house."

"What is his name?" demanded the Yankee, dipping his quill into the ink.

"Jacinto Delacruz of Santa Fe."

As the man wrote his name, Jacinto stood frozen with shock. *Live with old Señora Gomez!*

But what Don Quirino said next shocked him even more. "I bid you welcome to Rancho San Bernardino and hope you will prosper here. You have made a contract with me and I with you. I will send you goats and pigs, and you may keep twenty of my mules. The rest shall be delivered to my corral. I suggest to each of you that you do not try to leave my rancho. The man or woman who leaves without my permission I will consider a thief because he has taken gifts from me. *Adios*."

Aldama spoke to his cowboys. They wheeled their horses about in a body, leaving Ross folding the paper Santos Gamboa had just signed. Jacinto handed the reins to the Yankee, who didn't even look at him.

"Take your people a mile down the river," Ross

said to Gamboa, "I will meet you there." Then he
heaved himself, grunting, into the saddle and rode off,
his legs and arms flapping. Jacinto knew he didn't like
the American who had put his name down on the paper
and who rode so badly. But even more he hated Santos
Gamboa, who had tricked him.

"I do not want to live with the old Gomez woman,"
he told Gamboa. "You did not say anything about that
when we were on the Trail."

"No," Gamboa agreed, "but her husband was alive
then. I had not expected him to die. He was not as old
as she is. She needs your help now. She cannot return
to New Mexico. It is your duty as a good Christian
to help her."

"I am not a Christian," Jacinto said angrily. "I am
a Comanche. I did not listen to that old priest in
Santa Fe."

Gamboa's voice was cold. "So Padre Luna complained to me. And I have noticed on the Trail that
you did not pray once with us. If you did not listen
to him, that is your business, and you may someday
regret it. But you will not insult our faith. You will
live with Señora Gomez as I have said."

Jacinto protested, "I do not have to stay here!"

"No, you do not. But consider the bears and snakes
and the Utes—and Aldama's men—if you try to cross
the mountains. And do not think to journey to the

west. There are no pueblos between here and Los
Angeles. Afoot you will be attacked by wild bulls of
the cattle herds."

"I can take a mule," Jacinto raged at the man, heed-
less of the New Mexicans listening to their argument.

"Aldama's mules have his brand on them. Every
ranchero between here and Los Angeles knows that
brand as well as he knows his own. Aldama will get
you back."

"Why would Aldama want me if he knew I didn't
want to stay?"

Gamboa gazed up into the cottonwoods where black
ravens were fighting each other. "Don Quirino's land
grant was given to him by the Government of Mexico.
To keep the grant he must always have a certain
number of people on his land. He has as much need
of us as we have of him. To him you are only a number,
but because you are a number you are important. Do
you understand what I am saying to you?"

Jacinto spun on his heel to walk away, but Gamboa
caught him by the collar of his shirt, ripping it as he
jerked him back. He gave the boy a shove that sent
him flying against the trunk of a tree. "You will not
make trouble for me here. You will live with the
Widow Gomez and work as we work. To see that you
do this you will be watched again. Do you understand?"

The Comanche boy wouldn't speak. For a time he
glared, then he nodded, thinking that living in Santa

Fe had been better than what California promised. At least in New Mexico he did not have to be a farmer.

The land Aldama gave to the settlers delighted them. The donated fields bordered the river, which the American agent called the Santa Ana. It would be a simple matter to irrigate the fields from the river's water, according to farmers among the New Mexicans. Men who had been hunters were pleased with the game they found in California. Pronghorn antelope ran twice across the path of Gamboa's caravan before they had traveled the Yankee mile Ross had set up as the correct distance. Quail and rabbits sprang up out of the grass in every direction ahead of them. Many of the birds were unknown and their calls strange to the New Mexicans, but a roadrunner hastened in front of Señora Gamboa's mule, making her laugh at its familiar outstretched head and body.

For his village Gamboa chose a flat piece of ground facing toward sharp brown mountains. It was not far from the river and backed by a bluff. Across the Santa Ana was another bluff. He called the town-to-be Agua Mansa—Gentle Water—and gentle the river seemed to be. The New Mexicans would start to build their homes at once, and from them they would go out to the fields. For a time, though, they would have to live in lean-tos, or ramadas, booths of brush and tree branches. New Mexicans had no need of California

Indians to teach them how to build ramadas. The sulking Jacinto was sent with Hipolito and several other men to the river to hack branches from trees. Others carried the branches to the town site, and still others set up the open-face shelters. By nightfall enough ramadas had been built to house the settlers and their families. Gamboa ordered Jacinto to put his bedding and other belongings in the ramada constructed for Carmela Gomez. He added, "You will not be sorry you have helped her. She was one of the finest cooks in Taos."

"Am I to hunt for her?" Jacinto asked, feeling very clever. If he hunted he'd be given a musket, though he'd never fired one. With a musket he might be able to escape.

"No, we have men who will hunt for fresh meat for everyone. You will make adobes."

Jacinto's anger rose higher. "I am a Comanche. I will make myself a bow and arrows."

"Do as you please later, but first make adobes."

If there was anything in the world Jacinto detested, it was making adobe bricks. He'd made them only once before when Delacruz had decided a wall needed repairing. The boy had done the job with such ill grace that the other servants refused to work with him. Jacinto had been whipped and put to work scouring kitchen kettles instead.

Santos Gamboa went off almost at once with the

mules Aldama had asked to be returned to him. He came back with two straw-filled oxcarts driven by California Indians. They looked at the New Mexicans without much interest, unloaded their straw, and headed again for Aldama's ranch.

There would be no tile or wooden floors in Agua Mansa, only dirt. Gamboa set the women to driving mules over the earth that children had cleared of grass and bushes. While the mules tamped the ground to hardness, the men and boys, Jacinto among them, dug clay out of the banks of the river, mixed it with straw as a binder, formed it into bricks, and laid them aside to dry in the hot autumn sun.

Each householder would build his own one-story house as he saw fit, to suit the size of his family. Gamboa spoke with the Yankee Ross, who sent several cartloads of planks to Agua Mansa. Because there was no saw-mill on the Rancho San Bernardino, the planks had been hand-sawn. This precious wood was for the door lintels and the roof beams. When the beams were laid in place on top of the adobes, men filled the spaces in between the planks with tules from the swamps. Then Gamboa went to Aldama again and asked for tar for the roof and received barrels of it, transported from the tar pits near Los Angeles. Over the tar went a layer of adobe and over the walls a thin coat of rainproof brown plaster smoothed on by everyone, even by the children, who loved to work with the gummy mess.

Agua Mansa was built in the form of a square in the New Mexican fashion with a small plaza in the center. Jacinto had to admit that the house of the Widow Gomez was no better or no worse than anyone else's, in spite of his unwilling work under Hipolito's watchful eyes. Many skilled settlers had helped him build it. Like the other houses, it had a small, round indoor fireplace, an outside adobe oven, and shutters made of cowhide, another gift from Aldama. Certainly the widow's house was not the equal of the fine Delacruz house, but it was comfortable enough, and the old woman was very pleased with it and her field.

The New Mexicans worked frantically. In a few weeks' time everyone was housed in an adobe building and the abandoned ramadas burned for firewood. Jacinto knew by the end of November why Gamboa had been in such a hurry. Like the others, the boy had heard that there would never be snow in this part of California but there would be rain. If it had rained before the settlers had roofed and plastered their homes, the houses would have melted under furious rainfall. Rain could come pelting down in California, everyone soon learned. As it was, after four days of rain Jacinto noticed that although the river rose in its bed, the hastily built houses stood fast.

His anger undiminished at having to work making adobes and building the Gomez house, Jacinto stood in the doorway of his new home one morning early in

December, watching as Don Quirino Aldama, Ross, and some *vaqueros* came riding to inspect the finished village. Following them were three oxcarts driven by California Indians and filled with livestock for Gamboa's settlers. The Indians distributed goats, pigs, and chickens to anyone who came to the carts for them.

Señora Gomez sent a sullen Jacinto after a milk goat, a shoat to raise, and a half dozen chickens. After some weeks of living in her house, Jacinto didn't hate the old woman but he didn't like her either. She talked too much, and she persisted in considering him much younger than he was. Her *tortillas* were light and her chili well-spiced, but the childish tales she continually told him bored him. She even told him of Juan de Oso, the boy who was half-bear, half-boy. And she had some queer ideas that unruly children were dragged away in the night by hairy-bodied monsters and that wicked people turned into beetles when they died. One night when Jacinto had a toothache, she prayed to Santa Apolonia for him, and when lightning flashed during a rainstorm in the mountains, she went down on her knees to beg Santa Clara for protection. Jacinto himself admitted he didn't like the lightning, but then no Comanche did.

The Widow Gomez was old and a fool and he'd give much to escape from her and Agua Mansa, but there was never a chance. On Santos Gamboa's order, one of the New Mexican men seemed to have his eyes on

Jacinto day and night. When he went to the river to hunt for the right wood to make his bow and arrows, Hipolito accompanied him.

The fact that Agua Mansa had no church pleased Jacinto, who refused to take part in Gamboa's outdoor worship. Each Sunday morning that winter Gamboa led his settlers in prayer on the place near the river where he'd decided to build their church when a priest came to them.

One Sunday morning, only days before Christmas, while Gamboa and the settlers were at their services, two strangers rode into the settlement: one on a roan, the other on a saddleless black mule. Jacinto, who sat on a tree stump in the plaza, shaping an arrow shaft with his knife, was the first New Mexican to see them. He got up, undecided whether to call Gamboa or not. The first stranger was an old man with long white hair streaming from under a beaver hat. He carried a long rifle and wore fringed buckskin and moccasins. Though he dressed like a Plains Indian, he was a white man with bright blue eyes. The other rider was a thin boy near Jacinto's age. Whether the boy was Mexican or not Jacinto couldn't tell. His black hair was shoulder-length like a Mexican's, but his shirt of rough wool, his bolero of sheepskin, and moccasins instead of high-heeled boots made Jacinto wonder about him.

The old white man said in the worst Spanish Jacinto had ever heard, "My name is Joshua Dove. I been up in the mountains after cabibs and only jes now got back. My wife and Teodoro here who was visitin' her told me you folks had got here from New Mexico. Has Aldama treated you right? Do you need anythin'? Where's Gamboa?"

Jacinto thought he understood the strange Spanish. He guessed the old man wanted to know if Don Quirino had treated the settlers well—not him personally. He nodded and pointed toward the river, wondering what "cabibs" were.

"I'm obliged to ya, boy." The old man rode past Jacinto toward the river, leaving Teodoro behind.

Teodoro seemed to be something of a mind reader as he grinned and said, "Cabibs are what he calls grizzly bears. That's what old Señor Dove hunts and all he really cares about. He's the finest hunter of bears in all California, even if he hunts them the Yankee way instead of the way the *vaqueros* do."

Bewildered by this strange conversation, all Jacinto could say was, "He's old to hunt bears, isn't he?" Not even Comanche men hunted buffalo when they were as old as Joshua Dove.

"Don't say that to him. Who are you?" asked Teodoro.

Jacinto thought, then said, "They call me Jacinto here, but my name is Spotted Wild Horse. I am a Comanche. Who are you?"

"Teodoro Ramirez. My grandmother and mother

and father were Serrano Indians, but my grandfather was born in Mexico. He is Carlos Ramirez, who was caretaker for the padres before the Aldama family came."

"Padres? Priests?" asked Jacinto.

Teodoro nodded, swinging his feet, tickling the withers of the mule with his moccasins. "This land belonged to the church and was part of the Mission San Gabriel. That was when Spain ruled California. When the Mexicans threw the Spaniards out of Mexico, they drove the priests out of California, too. I was very small then. There are no missions anymore."

"Will the priests return?"

Teodoro shook his head. "Not to the missions. Grandfather says there will be churches in this valley, though. Will you New Mexicans build a church here?"

Jacinto smiled. "*They* will build a church. I do not care for churches. When I lived in Santa Fe, I liked only one thing about churches—their bells. Everyone liked the bells of the churches there."

Teodoro said, "I have never heard a bell, but I know what they are. My grandfather talks of the church bells he listened to each day when he was a young man in Mexico. I have never gone into a church that I can remember." Teodoro was grinning. "Do you like anything else besides bells, Spotted Wild Horse?"

"I like horses!"

"Have you seen the herds of the Aldamas?"

"No," Jacinto frowned. "I haven't seen their horses or their cattle. I haven't done anything but make adobes and build pens for sheep, goats, and pigs."

The Ramirez boy's face was somber. "Perhaps I will ask Serafin to lend horses to you and me and take us soon to find one of the horse herds. Can you ride?"

Jacinto scoffed. "You do not know Comanches if you ask such a thing. Who is Serafin?"

"Serafin Aldama. El Chino. He is my very good friend."

TEODORO

IV

Although Joshua Dove, the Yankee bear hunter, interested Jacinto, Teodoro interested him even more. He was the only boy he had met in California so near his own age, and Teodoro claimed to be a friend of the remarkable El Chino, who might lend horses to people he liked.

Jacinto had come to California to see the horse herds, not to be a farmer in the mud village of Agua Mansa. But there was no escaping the watchfulness of the New Mexicans. Even the Widow Gomez seemed to Jacinto to keep an eye on him, asking him to bring water from the river for her or to find her strayed shoat and put it in the pen, safe from coyotes. He hated doing errands for her. He detested the chickens that tried to wander into her house to lay eggs wherever they pleased and disturbed him when he worked on his arrows.

He knew that when time came to start planting he would hate life on Rancho San Bernardino even more. He didn't mind so much digging irrigation canals or helping place willow stakes as fences between the individual fields. Such things were man's work at least. But weeding and hoeing the Widow Gomez's field would not be a Comanche man's work at all. Weeding was the labor of women and of children. And so was keeping birds away from the crops. But Señora Gomez was too old to do these chores for herself. All she was good for was to annoy him, chattering about bad dreams and claiming ghosts had touched her. But she made better *tortillas* than he'd eaten in Santa Fe.

While Jacinto waited, bored, for Teodoro to come visiting again, Gamboa and the other settlers argued about the proper time to plant in California where the seasons were so different. January was a month for snow in northern New Mexico, but Aldama's *vaqueros* had never seen snow except in the mountains. Rain they knew and disliked. It rained much in January in California, but the New Mexicans need not fear snow, Don Quirino himself had told them. Finally after much talk, then conferring with Joshua Dove, who had lived in Californa for many years, Gamboa decided they would plant their corn, beans, peppers, and squash in late March. They hoped that seeds brought from New

Mexico would grow here, but some settlers shook their heads doubtfully. Planting in March meant that the fields must be made ready in February, cleared of brush and rocks, and everyone agreed that California soil was very rocky.

Three days of this back-breaking labor decided Jacinto on a new course. Santos Gamboa had accepted his word when he'd promised on the journey that he wouldn't run away. Perhaps the man would be convinced by the fact that he hadn't tried to. Gamboa might accept his word again if he offered to stay in exchange for something Jacinto wanted.

He sought out Gamboa where he sat in the plaza at twilight, cleaning his musket. "May I speak with you?" Jacinto was careful to use Spanish.

"Sí, Jacinto." Gamboa didn't smile at him as he did at the other young people. Jacinto felt the man's wariness.

"I don't want to work in the field of Señora Gomez." Before Gamboa could become angry, Jacinto hurried on. "I was a house servant. I have never harnessed an ox or mule or used a plow. I will work, though. I want to herd the goats and sheep. I could be a shepherd again."

"And run away the moment you are out of sight of the village?"

"No." Jacinto folded his arms. "I told you once

before that I wouldn't run away, and I kept my promise. I have changed my mind. I will stay here if I can be a shepherd."

The man nodded. "Sí, you did stay. But if you are to guard the animals, you will need weapons."

"I have made myself a bow and arrows and a quiver. I am not asking you for a musket."

"Show them to me."

Jacinto ran back to the Gomez house and took his possessions out from under his blankets that were rolled into a corner. As he left, the old woman seated on a stool before the fire gave him a strange look. "Are you running away and leaving me, Jacinto?"

"You will be looked after if I do." Jacinto paid no heed to her sigh. He went back to the plaza and displayed his bow to the other Comanche. Jacinto knew he'd done well even if he didn't have Osage orange for the bow and dogwood for the shafts of his arrows. He'd used the woods he'd found in California, deer sinews, and granite from which he had fashioned arrow tips. The quiver was of deer hide.

Gamboa looked everything over carefully, then spoke to Jacinto for the first time in Comanche. "They are well done. I would not have thought you could remember how to make them the Comanche way."

The boy said proudly, "I did not forget. Big Wolf of the Honey Eaters is my father."

Gamboa switched to Spanish. "I have heard his name. He is a chief, but Comanches mean little here in California."

"Were you taken captive, too?" Jacinto asked.

"I was taken in a raid when I was seven years old and sold to a man in Abiquiu."

"Was he a good *patrón*?"

"He was. When he died some years ago, I was set free and became a trader."

"My *patrón* was not so kind," said Jacinto, "and his son was my enemy."

Gamboa's face bore no expression. "It happens sometimes that way. *Sí*, you may herd our flocks while others work the land. Do you know that it may be dangerous to be a shepherd and that you must not go too far from the village?"

Jacinto smiled. "The Yankee Señor Dove says bears might come down from the mountains to raid your fields."

Gamboa didn't smile. "No one knows as much of bears as Don Joshua, who was once a mountain man and fur trader. I have known him a long time. He is our good friend."

"The Yankee Ross is not so good a friend," Jacinto said flatly. Ross had come several times to Agua Mansa but not with gifts from Aldama. It seemed even to Señora Gomez that Aldama's agent was keeping a sharp eye on things. As for Don Quirino, neither he nor the wondrous El Chino had appeared again, nor had the friendly Teodoro Ramirez.

Gamboa didn't discuss Ross. "Tomorrow, then, take the animals downstream. Tell the Widow Gomez you are to be a herdsman and her land will be farmed by others. I will see that she is not cheated."

"*Sí*." Jacinto flung his arrow-filled quiver over his shoulder, turned on his heel, and went to the corral below the bluff to inspect it for strength. He would be responsible for all the goats and sheep of Agua Mansa, which was an important job. And if he was lucky, he might see the horse herds of the Aldamas running free on the plain.

Jacinto led the animals out at daybreak ten days in a row before he got his wish. He'd seen cattle wandering singly and in little groups beside the river and had once been an object of curiosity to a wild, longhorned steer. When Jacinto had thrown a rock at it, the animal lumbered off over the edge of one of the many gullies thereabouts.

Fortunately for the goats and sheep—and for himself—Jacinto was near another gully when the horses finally came running from the south. The rains had stopped five days before and the weather turned hot. The boy's first warning of the horses was the cloud of yellow dust on the horizon. When he bent to the ground and heard the thudding of hooves, he shouted at the sheep and goats and, pushing them with a stick, drove them down a path into the gully. From there Jacinto readied his bow, putting an arrow into it. He waited, his gaze fixed on the rim of the gully.

To his joy the horses swept along it, unaware of his presence. They were magnificent, these California horses, large and fleet and of every color a horse might be. Chestnut, roan, sorrel, white, gray, black—even pinto, the horse Comanches favored above all others. Led by a gray ghost of a stallion, the herd of a hundred or more animals raced along the edge of the gully, then suddenly swerved and galloped east.

Jacinto came out with his animals when he felt it was safe and the horses wouldn't return. Their dust had blown away, though the marks of their hooves were still clear in the dusty earth. He was delighted that he had seen them, but seeing them only made his wish for a horse of his own stronger.

Perhaps if he behaved well and never lost a sheep or goat, Santos Gamboa would permit him to visit Teodoro and they would talk of horses. Joshua Dove, who came often to Agua Mansa, would tell him where Teodoro lived. Jacinto would ride a mule there. It would never do to appear on foot, not when Teodoro had come riding.

March and most of April came and went. The settlers planted the seeds from New Mexico and prepared to grow three kinds of corn—blue for *tortilla* flour, red and yellow for food, and white for the mules. The land beside the Santa Ana was good land. Nearly every seed planted took root. Grapevines pushed up through the soil, delighting the settlers who wanted to make wine. Jacinto passed by the grapes with a superior air. Comanches had no use for wine or for whiskey, which they called "fool's water."

One warm day in late April Jacinto rested on a fallen cottonwood beside the river, watching his goats climbing up and down on an outcropping of rock. He thought about the broadness of Comanche lands and contrasted them with California. Of course, California had no buffalo. The cattle and horses ran free over the countryside, the animals of one rancho mingling with those of another. But here the land was owned by only a few men whereas in Comanche country no Indian owned the land itself. How different the Mexicans and the Comanches were! The Mexicans built houses on their land and didn't move from place to place. Although Comanches moved constantly, their horses didn't run free. As for cattle, Comanches didn't bother with them at all. Jacinto pondered the queer California way of doing things.

The Yankee Ross had come to Agua Mansa the evening before and had told the settlers that Don Quirino's *vaqueros* would be hunting for unbranded cattle and spring calves in a week's time. The settlers must not hinder the work of Aldama's men if they appeared in the village and fields, or Don Quirino would be very displeased. Santos Gamboa had promised Ross that his New Mexicans would not interfere with the roundup of the cattle.

Carmela Gomez wasn't happy, though, with Gamboa's promise. Riders had invaded her father's fields once in New Mexico and trampled the spring corn when she'd been a girl. Jacinto had listened to her complaints between the blows of her stone pestle pounding into the mortar as she prepared cornmeal. "*Ay de mí*, there is no flour mill so I must work too hard for my old bones. And now we must bear this—*vaqueros* riding across our fields. And if we dare complain, Don Quirino will surely not get a priest for us. *Ay de mí!*"

"A priest?" Jacinto had pricked up his ears at this word.

"*Sí*, Gamboa has asked Don Quirino through that Yankee Ross to write and ask for a priest to come to us."

The boy said quickly, "There is no church."

"When we have our priest, we will build a church for him. I have thought often of a church." Jacinto saw the old woman's eyes glance at the carved wooden *santos* figure hanging from a cord on the wall. She favored San Isidro, the patron of the fields. "Each night, Jacinto," she said, "I pray to San Isidro and Santa Barbara to send us a priest and help us build a church. The land is already chosen for it, fine land beside the river that is so gentle."

The boy muttered, "I didn't know this."

"Jacinto Delacruz, you do not come to worship with us, so how could you know? There is where we speak of the church that is to be and of getting a fine bell for it someday."

Sitting on the cottonwood eating a *tortilla*, Jacinto now thought about the possibility of a priest coming to Agua Mansa. A priest meant not only Mass on Sundays and other days of the week, he probably meant a school, too. And Santos Gamboa struck him as the sort of man who'd force him to go to school as well as to Mass. Jacinto had resisted school in Santa Fe, though he had learned to read and write a little Spanish. He tore off a piece of *tortilla* and threw it at one of the nearby yellow-eyed goats, then yelled at the animal, "If Gamboa does that, I will run away over the mountains and take as many California horses with me as I can. The Aldamas won't catch Spotted Wild Horse."

Teodoro Ramirez came to Jacinto's village the next Sunday, arriving again while the settlers were at the riverside, worshipping. Jacinto was very pleased to see him, though he only nodded when Teodoro got off his mule and came over to him, where he squatted against the wall of the Gomez house. Jacinto had learned from talking with Joshua Dove that Serranos were a group of California Indians. Teodoro was three-quarters Serrano and one-quarter Mexican. That one-quarter could be overlooked, Jacinto had decided. Teodoro interested him. The other boys in Agua Mansa did not; they were too young or too old, and they were at heart farmers like their fathers.

Teodoro tethered the mule to the side of a cart and squatted in the shade beside Jacinto, who was watching ravens stalking over the dirt of the plaza. "Tell me of Comanches. Tío Carlos says he has heard the name, but he hasn't known any Comanches."

"Who is Tío Carlos?"

"My grandfather. Everyone calls him Uncle Carlos because he is so old."

"Does he know Santos Gamboa?"

Teodoro scratched his head. "The man who brought you here over the mountains? I think if Tío Carlos doesn't know him, Gamboa would surely know Tío Carlos. Everybody knows us."

"Santos Gamboa used to be a Comanche," Jacinto said. "But he is a Genizaro now."

Teodoro looked puzzled until Jacinto explained the meaning of the name. "But you say you're a Comanche, not a Genizaro?"

"I am. I'm Spotted Wild Horse, the son of Big Wolf, a chief of the band of Honey Eaters."

"If you're a chief's son, what are you doing here?"

Teodoro was a willing listener to Jacinto's story of how he was captured in Mexico, of the Delacruz family and the false accusation, of Gamboa and the journey.

"Do you want to go back to your tribe?" asked Teodoro.

"Yes."

"And they are far away from California?"

Jacinto pointed to the east. "Very far away."

Teodoro picked up a piece of straw and drew a line in the dust. "But, Spotted Wild Horse, you can't go back to them. See, this line I make is the eastern San Bernardino Mountains. Beyond them are badlands. Many men have tried to cross them and died. And beyond them is a very great desert. Tío Carlos crossed it when he came from Mexico many years ago. He saw there the bodies of men who had died of thirst. They dry up and become like men made of leather. It is very far from here to the Colorado River, where you find water once you've crossed this desert."

Jacinto had decided that he didn't know Teodoro well enough to entrust him with his plans to escape someday. He asked, "Have you ever fought the Utes?"

"No, but my grandfather did when the rancho of the Aldamas was part of Mission San Gabriel. He fought the Yumas and Mojaves, too, when they came here."

"There are many tribes in California?"

"Many, and all like horses to ride or to eat. Are there many tribes in the land of the Comanches?"

Jacinto was boastful. "Comanches do not willingly share their land or their buffalo herds with others."

"I have never seen a buffalo," murmured Teodoro. "Is it like a cow or a horse?"

"Neither," said Jacinto. He spoke of the herds he'd remembered seeing as a little boy and of the wandering life of his people.

"I think I know what a buffalo looks like now. Will you become a buffalo hunter, Spotted Wild Horse?"

"*Sí*, what will you be?"

"A *vaquero* for Don Quirino. Already I use a *reata* well and can ride. Can you handle a *reata*?"

"No, I do not know of *reatas*. House servants in Santa Fe don't use lariats. I will learn, though."

It was Teodoro's turn to boast. "California *vaqueros* are the best and bravest in the world."

"I do not think they can be better with horses than a Comanche, Teodoro. No one can tame a wild horse as a Comanche can."

"How do they tame horses?" Teodoro listened politely while Jacinto told him, then suddenly asked, "Do you own a horse yet?"

"No." Jacinto didn't like the question. "Santos Gamboa has a white mare. She is not a fine horse."

"Tío Carlos and I have only a mule to ride. We do

not need an ox because we are not farmers. We do not have a rancho."

"If you do not have a rancho and you do not farm, how do you live?" asked Jacinto.

"Don Quirino gives Tío Carlos a pension. The Aldamas own the land our house is built upon. Do you own land?"

Jacinto laughed. "The Widow Gomez has her field and this house. I do not own anything but the weapons that I made and my bedding and clothing. That is all a Comanche man needs—and a horse."

Teodoro snatched at one of Carmela Gomez's hens as she went by, making the bird squawk. He held the hen to his breast and blew into her feathers while she fluttered in fury. "We have some pigs and a dog and chickens." With a sudden motion, the boy released the hen. Watching her totter off angrily, Teodoro laughed and said, "Some of the birds we have aren't ordinary chickens. You should come see them."

"All chickens are ordinary. They cackle, crow, or lay eggs, Teodoro."

Teodoro had a sly, crooked smile. "Not these. They are gamecocks. They fight. I have some half-grown birds. Tío Carlos and I will train them for the cock-fights."

Jacinto had heard of cockfighting in Santa Fe but had never seen a match. "How does anyone train a chicken? They are too stupid."

"It is done," the other boy said calmly. "Sometimes Tío Carlos and I win betting."

"I would like to see a cockfight," said Jacinto.

"You may be able to come when the Aldamas have their next *fiesta*. Probably they will ask Santos Gamboa."

"He wouldn't go. He'd be afraid a coyote might eat a ripening grape if he went away."

Teodoro chuckled. "So that is how farmers think?" Then he said suddenly, "Spotted Wild Horse, I would like to give you a gamecock."

"Why?"

"Because you have no horse and Tío Carlos and I have eight gamecocks. I will give you the one we call El Cobarde. He is mine."

Jacinto grinned. "You name a little chicken the Coward?"

"When you see him you will know why. We think El Cobarde may be crazy."

"A crazy chicken? And you want me to have him. I don't know how to keep a gamecock, Teodoro."

"Men here in Agua Mansa will tell you."

Jacinto shook his head slowly. "Santos Gamboa would not like it."

"Is he your *patrón*?"

"No, he says he is not, even though he could be. My *patrón* in Santa Fe gave me to him but he signed no paper." Jacinto traced circles in the dust next to the drawing Teodoro had made of the mountains and the desert.

"If he is not your *patrón*, it is your business where you go and what you own." Teodoro got up. "When Gamboa comes from the river I will give him greetings from my grandfather and ask that you be permitted to go with me to our house today to visit. The mule can carry both of us."

Somewhat to Jacinto's surprise, Gamboa said he could go but he must be back before nightfall in the Widow Gomez's house. Jacinto sensed from the tone of the man's voice that he didn't much approve of Teodoro, though he'd seemed pleased that old Carlos Ramirez was well. Jacinto thought Gamboa gave Teodoro something of the same look he'd given Aldama's youngest son, El Chino.

Riding on the old black mule behind Teodoro wasn't Jacinto's idea of riding at all, not even when Teodoro obligingly went out of his way to visit *vaqueros* moving about in the distance. When they were close enough, Jacinto saw that the cowboys were skinning steers. The bodies of flayed steers, glistening white and red, were scattered over the plain. But there were no women cutting up the beef, which was the Comanche way with buffalo. One man on horseback came galloping up, while the *vaqueros* worked, and began to shout orders at them. "What are they doing? What of the flesh of the cattle?" Jacinto asked his new friend.

Teodoro laughed. "This is the time of the *matanza*. Don Quirino's cowboys have slaughtered the full-grown steers with lances. Now they skin them for the hides. The Yankee traders in Los Angeles will buy the skins after they have been stretched for two days. The Yankees will pay two American dollars for each hide."

Jacinto shook his head. "Comanches use every part of the buffalo."

"That is not how Californios deal with cattle, but if the people of Agua Mansa came to take meat and dry it, I doubt if Don Quirino would care." Teodoro called out "*Adios*" to the cowboys, turned the mule about, and the boys headed back toward the river. A hundred yards from the cowboys the old mule stopped in its tracks. Jacinto looked down wondering if it feared walking over a patch of gopher holes. And then he saw the thick, dust-colored snake under a bush, coiled to strike, its tongue flicking in and out, its rattles buzzing.

"Do not move," Teodoro whispered. "The *vaqueros* will know something is wrong when they see that we do not move, and one of them will come."

Jacinto sat motionless, his foot dangling far too close to the rattlesnake for him to feel at ease. The cowboys would carry pistols as all California *vaqueros* did, but how good were they at shooting? And at such a distance?

As Teodoro had predicted, a *vaquero* came—but not

with a pistol. Jacinto heard a thunder of swift hoof-beats. Afraid to turn his head to see what the cowboy would do, the Comanche boy saw only the lightning-swift flick of the edge of the circle of rawhide that grazed his right moccasin and the sudden collapse of the snake into a mass of bloody coils. The Californian had used his *reata* as a teamster would use his bullwhip!

Jacinto looked over his shoulder and saw the laughing *vaquero* pulling back his *reata*, recoiling it to loop over his saddle peg.

"*Gracias*," Teodoro told him calmly.

"It was nothing, boy," remarked the *vaquero* before he trotted back to the skinning, leaving Jacinto vowing to himself that tomorrow he'd start to practice with a *reata*. He never had heard of a Comanche killing a snake with a *reata*!

The house of Tío Carlos had been built years before the village of Agua Mansa, and it had not been well kept. The first thing Jacinto saw in the one-room house was a bucket standing under a hole in the roof, placed there days before to catch rain. This house was much like that of the Widow Gomez, but not at all as neat. The dirt floor hadn't been swept in a long time. A goat was asleep on an old red blanket in a corner. The Widow Gomez would never permit a goat in her house, which smelled only of chili and garlic.

An old man was sitting on a stool, braiding leather thongs with his old brown hands. He was white-haired and shrunken, dressed as Teodoro was in a shirt, trousers, and sheepskin bolero.

"Tío Carlos," said Teodoro, "I have brought the Comanche, Spotted Wild Horse."

"You are welcome. My house is your house," said the old man.

Jacinto bowed as he knew Teodoro would want him to. Truly, Tío Carlos was ancient, but his dark eyes were unlike the lizard eyes of many old people. They were bright like a squirrel's. "Santos Gamboa sends you greetings," Jacinto said.

"Sí, I have been told by Don Joshua that he came over the mountains with many people."

"Grandfather, I want to show Spotted Wild Horse our gamecocks. I want to give him El Cobarde."

Tío Carlos chuckled dryly. "El Cobarde? Sí."

Teodoro led the way behind the adobe and the rickety corral, where he'd put the mule, to a row of rough cages made of wood and brush and held together with rawhide thongs. "Gamecocks must be kept separate. As soon as they cease to be chicks, one will surely kill the other. They are like wild bulls from different herds."

"Where is El Cobarde?"

Teodoro went the opposite way toward a tree on the other side of the house. There Jacinto saw a small rooster, hunkered down in the dust, a bundle of feathers. He wasn't a handsome bird as far as Jacinto could see. Under all the dust he was probably an unattractive, yellowish-white color.

Teodoro whistled. The bird got up, walked to the length of the string tied around one foot, tilted his head, and looked expectantly at Jacinto. Then he tried to fly up onto Teodoro's shoulder, but the string was too short. The bird rubbed himself against Teodoro's leg.

"You see, he is loco. Tío Carlos and I think El Cobarde thinks he is a dog. He is too friendly. He keeps company with the dog." Teodoro pointed to a small brown dog, head on its paws, sleeping in the shade. "El Cobarde is like that. He lies down when he sees another gamecock. Tío Carlos will not bother to train this one who refuses to fight."

"But what am I to do with such a bird, Teodoro?"

"Take him out of my sight. Cook him if you want to. We bred him from fighting cocks. Don Quirino gave you New Mexicans some hens. Perhaps El Cobarde's chicks will become good fighters."

"Why don't you cook him?" Jacinto asked, eyeing the rooster dubiously.

"Tío Carlos says it would be like cooking our dog. But El Cobarde is young enough to be tender."

Jacinto shrugged. "I will take him. Hipolito Gamboa may know something of gamecocks or the Widow Gomez may make chicken *empanadas* next Sunday."

"As you please, Spotted Wild Horse. I will give him

to you when we go back to Agua Mansa. Now come see the real gamecocks, the fine ones. Then we shall eat with my grandfather, who is the worst cook in all California."

"The Widow Gomez might be the best," Jacinto informed him.

Teodoro stopped walking. "Tío Carlos thinks only of gamecocks and making *reatas* for the Aldama family and of the mission priests, who are no longer here in the valley. He burns the frijoles every time but says he would never marry again."

"How often do you go to the Aldama rancho, Teodoro?"

"When someone tells us there is to be a *fiesta*. Don Quirino sends a cart for my grandfather, and we take our best gamecocks with us. There has never been a *fiesta* at the Aldama rancho without cockfighting. Everyone who has a bird brings him."

"And I could bring El Cobarde, who is loco?"

"Loco or no, El Cobarde is a gamecock. He will certainly be welcome and you with him, Spotted Wild Horse."

EL
COBARDE

V

El Cobarde had been quiet in Jacinto's arms as he and
Teodoro rode to the village at sunset, but the moment
they arrived the rooster gave a squawk and leaped out
of Jacinto's grasp. The boys watched him flap his way
up onto the edge of the rooftop of Carmela Gomez's
house.

"The other chickens frightened him," explained
Teodoro.

Jacinto saw how the hens had scattered, as frightened
as El Cobarde. Then Señora Gomez came out of her
house, attracted by all of the squawking. She stared up
at her roof where most of the noise was coming from
and saw the white rooster. When she turned to look

at Jacinto, to his surprise she was smiling. "Where did this gamecock come from?"

"He is mine," the boy told her defiantly.

"Well, then, get him down at once before he flies away."

Jacinto slid down from the mule while Teodoro, not taking his eyes from the old woman, said, "*Adios*. Good luck with the bird." He kicked the mule and left Agua Mansa as fast as he could. Plainly Teodoro was leaving Jacinto to deal with the worthless gamecock and the New Mexicans.

Jacinto climbed to the roof, but El Cobarde had no intention of being caught. He flew to the ground and stood flapping his wings not far from Señora Gomez. Jacinto watched her walk slowly and calmly toward the bird and heard her murmuring, "Come here. Come here, Blanquito." She picked up the rooster and started to stroke his dusty feathers. El Cobarde didn't struggle at all as he had at first when Jacinto picked him up. Jacinto got down off the roof, wondering.

"What was he named?" Señora Gomez asked, still holding the bird.

"El Cobarde."

She laughed. "I shall call him Blanquito—the little white one. With a name like El Cobarde he will never fight well."

"You do not want to cook him?"

"A very fine bird like this? He is heavy and hard as
a gamecock should be. I would not cook such a bird!"

"*You* know about gamecocks, *señora?*"

She smiled. "My husband bred them for many years.
Where do the Californians hold their mains? That is
what a cockfight is called."

"At Aldama's rancho." Jacinto was amazed at the old
woman. "Do you like the bird, *señora?*"

"*Sí,* I like him. I have always like gamecocks. We
shall keep this one and train him."

"I do not know how."

"So, you marvelous Comanches do not know about
gamecocks? Mexicans do, and my husband was Mexican. This bird must be fed certain foods, his body
massaged well, and he must be given much exercise
to make him swift and very strong."

In his excitement and surprise that the old woman
would know about gamecocks, Jacinto let the insulting
remark about Comanches pass. "But, *señora,* the bird
is a coward!"

"Bah, when the time comes for him to fight, to be
put to the main, I will put remarkable courage into
him. You will see."

During that very hot, dry summer Jacinto learned
what the woman meant about getting the bird ready
for cockfights. El Cobarde became as much her game-

cock as his. She had a cage built for him so he could stay in the house at night out of damp air rising from the river. He ate a diet of chopped eggs, raw meat, and cooked cornmeal. While Jacinto was shepherding animals, El Cobarde was collared and chased around and around the plaza for exercise by one or another of the small children who were not weeding the fields. For their trouble the Widow Gomez gave them candy made of brown sugar. Every night the gamecock was massaged by Jacinto so the bird's muscles would grow strong.

Soon the men of Agua Mansa took an interest in the rooster, even Santos Gamboa. They visited Señora Gomez to see how quickly the cock grew and to ask when he'd be ready for his first fight. Seeing how very respectfully they treated the old woman, Jacinto realized that she and her husband must have been well known in Taos as breeders of gamecocks. Men listened attentively when she spoke of famous cocks Jacinto never had heard of. Some of them had been of great value.

One night in September while Jacinto was massaging the bird, Santos Gamboa, Hipolito, and the Agua Mansa blacksmith came to the Gomez house. The smith had been especially invited.

"We shall need knives this long for Blanquito for his spurs," Señora Gomez explained to the man, showing him with her hands the length the blades were to be.

"Who will tie them?" asked Hipolito Gamboa.

"Jacinto will learn to do this. I will teach him."

The blacksmith nodded. "When will Blanquito be ready to be put to the main?"

"In two months' time when he is no longer moulting. I have made a sheath for his spurs. Jacinto holds him close to the rooster who belongs to the Perez family while I hold the Perez bird. Blanquito shows an interest in him."

Jacinto looked down into El Cobarde's feathers. The gamecock had tried a few feeble pecks at the other bird. That was all.

During the summer Teodoro had come three times to see how things fared with the white bird. He had smiled at Señora Gomez's efforts but was too polite to show his amusement. Everyone in Agua Mansa thought Tío Carlos permitted Teodoro too much freedom, but the boy had good manners, a trait that Mexicans valued.

Teodoro had brought news on his last visit. There would be a *fiesta* at the Aldama rancho in November. Don Quirino expected the head of his family to come visiting at that time from the pueblo of Los Angeles. Whenever old Don Pedro came to the rancho, a *fiesta* was held in his honor.

Jacinto spoke of the event to Santos Gamboa while Señora Gomez conferred with the blacksmith over the matter of the cock's knives. "There will be a *fiesta* before long at the Aldama rancho. I want to take this bird to it."

Gamboa nodded. "*Sí*, I have heard of the *fiesta*. You will go with me. I have business there."

Jacinto had hoped to go alone and have a good time. He listened sourly as the blacksmith asked, "What will you do there, Don Santos?"

"The Yankee Ross has told me that old Don Pedro may be able to get a priest for us. Old Aldama is a very important man in California. No priest has come in answer to our prayers. Perhaps Don Pedro will take a hand and get one for us. He has influence. It is said he journeys sometimes with a priest, who is his chaplain."

Jacinto hid his head in the rooster's feathers, making a face. Priests and churches—and weeds in the cornfields! Did Gamboa never think of anything more interesting? He never spoke of horses or even of Utes, though each night he posted guards armed with muskets in the fields and at the river that flowed by the village.

The boy wasn't really listening when the blacksmith said wistfully, "We left Santa Fe long ago and by now I should be accustomed to this village, but sometimes I miss the bells of Santa Fe."

"They were very fine," agreed Santos Gamboa, "the finest bells in all New Mexico."

Jacinto caught the word *bells*. Yes, he missed the

bells. Sometimes when he awoke early in the morning it seemed to him that he had heard them ringing.

Jacinto and the New Mexicans could hardly bear the gasping heat of the rest of September and early October. The Santa Ana, dependent on mountain streams and snows, shriveled between its banks of sand. The plain of Rancho San Bernardino became so dry that the earth cracked to powder under a man's sandals and dust puffed up when he walked. Dust eddied in small circles in the plaza while uprooted rustling tumbleweeds came bounding over the ground, terrifying Jacinto's goats and sheep as he drove them from place to place, looking for sweet grass in the shade.

Even though the rich soil of their fields had yielded fine crops of corn and grapes, the settlers muttered against the hot sun that beat hammerlike on them. Sweat came quickly but evaporated at once. The men wanted only to sit unmoving from noon until the sun had gone down. Harvesting in California had not been joyous work. Though the threshing of the peas and beans was done in the shade and the treading of grapes for wine accomplished under riverside trees, the work had been very hard in the heat. For his part Jacinto cursed the hot weather as he drove his flock over the threshing floor to harden it for the men who would do the threshing. Each day there was frantic work for everyone. Melons ripened daily, and the animals bawled constantly for water and for grass, which was not easily found.

If Jacinto had despised the life of a farmer before, he hated it even more now. Farmers were at the beck and call of the weather. How could a free Comanche like Santos Gamboa choose such a life? Surely Gamboa could have returned to his band and become a very respected buffalo hunter.

November came at last and with it welcome cooler days and nights. The Aldamas' *fiesta* promised to be favored by bright sunshine without real heat. Jacinto, as befitting a Comanche, tried not to show his excitement at the prospect of going to the rancho with El Cobarde. He'd seen the herds of horses three more times while he shepherded the sheep and goats about the countryside. His critical eye saw that each herd had been a different one and made up of many, many animals. Truly this was the Land of Many Horses.

Only Santos Gamboa and Jacinto went to the *fiesta*, though other settlers, according to a *vaquero* sent by Don Quirino, would be welcome. Gamboa had his "priest business" there, and the *vaquero* had assured Jacinto that he would be welcomed once he had shown El Cobarde, who had finished moulting and looked splendid. The Widow Gomez decided that she didn't want to go. A *vaquero* had left a hoofprint of his horse in the beans growing in a corner of her field. That had been done during the roundup of the calves and had been expected. But it had not made her feel kindly toward the Aldamas.

All the same she seemed pleased that Jacinto went. She fussed as much over him that morning as over El Cobarde. The boy had to wear his best trousers, a new shirt she'd embroidered for him, her husband's brightest serape, new sandals, and a straw hat. She wanted to trim his lengthening hair, but he wouldn't permit it. In fact, he combed his hair down the middle and drew a line of red paint along the part as Comanches did, which made her throw up her hands in despair.

El Cobarde had his comb cut short, his spurs trimmed, and his feathers shortened. The blacksmith had fashioned four-inch long blades to go over the rooster's spurs, and Señora Gomez had spent hours teaching Jacinto exactly how to bind the blades onto the stump of the natural spur with strong thread. El Cobarde was full grown now, a heavy and menacing-looking bird. But Jacinto worried. "What if he is a coward?"

"Bah," said the woman. "He will not refuse to fight." She gave Jacinto a little leather bag. "Before you put him to the main, feed Blanquito what is in here. Do not let any man see you do it."

"What is it, *señora?*"

"Courage. This courage was a secret of my husband's. His gamecocks always won. The other handlers will give courage to their birds also. Blanquito will not disgrace us."

Jacinto rode off with El Cobarde in his cage strapped to the saddle of a mule; Santos Gamboa rode on another. Together they went eastward over the plain to the Aldama ranch, some eight Yankee miles away. As they passed the great rocky hill men called Dove Mountain, where Joshua Dove's house lay in its shadow, the old bear hunter himself rode up to join them. With him came his wife, gray-haired Doña María, wearing a fringed shawl of black silk embroidered in far-off China with huge red roses.

The Comanche boy and the woman fell behind the two men. Because Señora Dove was silent, Jacinto listened to the talk of the old Yankee and Gamboa. Dove asked, "Did you fetch the bird along for the *corrida de gallos?*"

"The boy brings him for the cockfighting."

"Hm," said the old man, who already had peered at El Cobarde in his cage. "The bird looks fat and saucy to me. Maybe I'll bet on him and on the wild bull and any hoss El Chino rides. Ya know, Don Quirino captured hisself a big cabib last week, and his *vaqueros* brought in a bull from the range, the meanest un they could find. But that ain't why the wife and me go to the *fiesta*. We mostly go for fat cow and the hoss races."

"Fat cow?" asked Gamboa, sounding polite but confused.

"The grub. Bad grub's poor bull. Good grub's fat cow."

"Ah," said Gamboa.

The *fiesta* began to sound better and better to Jacinto—bear-and-bull fights, good food, and best of all horse racing. If El Chino was to race, surely the swiftest horses in all California would be there to compete.

"Gamboa, why are you goin' to the *fiesta?*" Dove asked a mile farther on.

"I wish to see Don Pedro Aldama about a priest for our village."

The Yankee grunted. "The old man'll be there. There's nothin' he likes better'n *fiestas* or hosses, 'cept mebbe his sons and grandsons. He's a mean old cuss though—thinks of hisself as a judge. When he was mayor of Los Angeles pueblo, he had two Mexican boys thrashed because they walked by him and didn' tip their hats to him."

Ah, thought Jacinto. Old Don Pedro seemed to be a man to avoid.

"I want nothing directly from Don Pedro or Don Quirino, only their help in getting a priest."

"Gamboa, you ain't fought no Utes yet for the Aldamas, so you ain't got no favors comin' from 'em."

"Don Joshua, it is no fault of mine that the Utes have not seen fit to raid Rancho San Bernardino since we have come."

"Well, that's fair enough," agreed Dove. "There's

no accountin' for the way Utes act. I seen 'em come month after month, and then they don' come for months. Mebbe that chief o' theirs, Walkara, knows you New Mexicans are here now."

"He may," Gamboa agreed. "Let us hope that will keep him away. All the same we watch for him and keep muskets and supplies ready."

"Tell that to Don Pedro."

"No, his son knows it well enough, I think. Don Quirino's agent keeps an eye on us."

Dove chuckled. "Ross'll git his money's worth outa ya, never you fear."

"We do not fear, Don Joshua."

The Aldama ranch house lay beyond a huge corral. Dove, his wife, Gamboa, and Jacinto left their animals in the corral with Aldama's Indian servants. Jacinto noticed how many very fine saddle horses were already there. He guessed correctly that Californians had ridden to the *fiesta* for miles from every direction.

Taking El Cobarde with him in the cage, Jacinto followed the others through the log gate that opened into the walled courtyard. The Aldama ranch house itself was so large it reminded Jacinto of the Palace of the Governors in Santa Fe. The house, too, was a fortress. The adobe walls surrounding it were nine feet high and had loopholes in them for muskets. The adobe house, which in some places formed part of the massive wall, was ninety feet long with very thick ten-foot-high walls and windows fitted with heavy wooden shutters. The house also had loopholes for guns. One room in the northwest corner, according to Joshua Dove, served as a chapel, and in the east wall Jacinto spied the painted plaster figure of a saint standing in a niche.

Jacinto had learned something of the history of Don Quirino's home from Teodoro. The house had been an *asistencia*, a chapel of San Gabriel Mission, built twenty years ago by Indian labor. No priest had lived in it, though Christian Indians stayed there and worked in the fields and vineyards. At times priests rode out from San Gabriel Mission to conduct Mass and to baptize and marry Indians. There had been attacks on the *asistencia* by hostile Indians, and many Christian Indians had been killed fighting the wild tribes from the desert. That was why the *asistencia* had been built as a fort and why the Aldama family, when the Government of Mexico drove out the mission priests and granted the Aldamas the rancho, maintained the house as a fortress. Who knew when the raiders would come again?

Jacinto looked around the large courtyard with curiosity. Many Californians had arrived already. Men and women were walking around the patio beside the fountain. As a former house servant, Jacinto knew that important people like the Doves would stay in the house as guests of Don Quirino. But he knew, too, that all guests, even the humblest, would have "fat cow," as Joshua Dove had put it. Jacinto could scent the good odor of chili and *puchero*, boiled corn and meat stew, from somewhere nearby and could see a whole beef being barbecued on a spit over a fire pit at one side of the courtyard. Indian menservants in white shirts were basting it with sauce from buckets set on the ground.

El Cobarde's sudden squawk when he heard another rooster crowing from over the wall made Joshua Dove turn around. "Jacinto, ya better find out where the gamecocks is kept. Ya'll find Tío Carlos there with 'em. Mosta the time the birds is to the west beside the Indian graveyard near the bullring Don Quirino built."

"*Gracias*, Señor Dove," said the Indian boy, turning around hastily to escape from view of the four men who were approaching them. One he recognized by his brown beard as Ross and another as Don Quirino. With Don Quirino walked a taller man with white hair and a white mustache. His face was square and severe, and his clothing, except for a white ruffled shirt, all black— Don Quirino's father, Jacinto guessed. At his side was a small round man in a long brown cassock.

Before the Doves and Gamboa were greeted by the men, Jacinto escaped through the gate with El Cobarde. There he came upon Teodoro, who was running from behind the western wall of the corral shouting, "Spotted Wild Horse! Spotted Wild Horse!"

There were more boys and men around the dusty outbuildings than in the beautiful Aldama courtyard, *vaqueros* and Indians and even fine *caballeros* looking around, some sitting under the olive trees playing *monte*, a card game. Jacinto felt more at home with them than with Don Quirino and his stern old father, who had boys thrashed for a small rudeness. Jacinto thought fleetingly of the Indian Santos Gamboa, wondering how much at ease he felt in the company of the Aldamas and the priest.

Teodoro was pulling wildly at Jacinto's arm. "Come see the bull and bear. Take El Cobarde to my grandfather. The cocks never fight until dark. El Chino is with the bull."

Jacinto kept his Comanche dignity in spite of his excitement as he took the rooster to Tío Carlos, who sat in a rawhide chair beside his gamecocks in their cages. Jacinto nodded politely and stood silently while the old man peered into the cage where El Cobarde drooped.

"The bird is heavier." Tío Carlos grinned, showing the teeth left to him. "You have trained him?"

"The Widow Gomez and I trained him."

The old Mexican laughed. "Trained by an old woman and a boy who knows nothing of gamecocks. That is right for such a worthless bird as this El Cobarde."

"Señora Gomez calls him Blanquito. She does not

like the name El Cobarde. If he is to be called by a name, we must call him Blanquito. Who will bet on a bird named El Cobarde?"

Tío Carlos shrugged. "As you please. He will be matched with other novice birds. I hope he will not disgrace your village."

"Señora Gomez says he will not." Jacinto felt for the leather bag inside his shirt. He must remember to give what was in it to the rooster.

Teodoro had been jumping up and down behind Jacinto all the while. Now his grandfather ordered irritably, "Go away, both of you. When you have seen everything there is to see and it is nightfall, come back. Until then, leave me in peace."

The boys hurried off together, Teodoro leading the way to a strong stockade of split logs on the east side of the ranch house. Peeking through a crack between logs, Jacinto, who had never seen a grizzly bear, grew wide-eyed at the enormous size of the animal prowling back and forth, then rising up on his hind legs, blinking his small eyes and snuffling.

"Now come see the bull," ordered Teodoro.

The bull, a great coppery-red animal with long wide horns, was in Aldama's bullring some distance from the log stockade. When they'd climbed to the top of the bullring, Jacinto saw to his excitement that El Chino was inside the ring, flapping a woman's purple shawl at the bull, annoying it. Suddenly the bull lowered his head and ran at El Chino, who dodged aside, laughing. Then he flung the shawl to a young *vaquero* waiting near the seats. Before the bull could skid to a stop in the dirt, turn around, and attack again, El Chino had jumped for the wall, grabbed it with both hands, and pulled himself up onto it.

Today he was truly magnificent. Without a hat or scarf his curly black hair gleamed in the sun. His jacket and trousers were the color of cow's cream and elaborately trimmed with black braid and gold buttons. Jacinto watched El Chino, his hands held behind his back, dance along the narrow adobe wall as if he were dancing at a *baile* with a pretty girl. The bull trotted along below him, his massive head lifted, looking up at the young man hopefully, waiting for him to fall.

El Chino disappointed the animal. When he came to the part of the wall where Teodoro and Jacinto stood, he stopped dancing and came over to them. "Who is this little one?" he asked Teodoro, pointing to Jacinto.

"Spotted Wild Horse. He is a Comanche Indian living in the village of the New Mexicans."

El Chino said, "I did not know that anyone from that village of farmers would come to our *fiesta*."

"The Comanche has brought a gamecock."

"*Sí*, that makes him welcome to my father." El Chino walked away to take the shawl from the *vaquero*, who waited with it.

"He has taken notice of you," Teodoro whispered to Jacinto. "I know he will take a fancy to you. When you get the chance, tell him what you told me about how Comanches break horses. That will interest him."

The rest of the first day of the *fiesta* went by swiftly for Jacinto and Teodoro, who alternated between watching entertainments put on by the *vaqueros* and stuffing themselves with food. They never went near the men and women dancing in the courtyard, though Jacinto enjoyed the music of the guitars more than he would show to Teodoro.

He and Teodoro were in the front of the crowd to see the horse racing held on the rolling land east of the ranch house. El Chino, mounted on various fine horses, almost always won when he started from a walk with the other riders at *"Santiago parado"* or at a sharp trot, *"Santiago andando."* At the yell of *"Santiago"* from Joshua Dove, who held the bettors' stakes, the horses began to gallop the course, pivoted, and returned like thunder. Jacinto wouldn't admit that the Californians rode better than Comanches, but their horses did surpass Indian ponies. How Jacinto longed to have a California horse of his own!

The *corrida de gallos* amazed him. He watched a barnyard rooster buried alive in the ground with only his head protruding. *Vaqueros* galloped down upon him, swooped low from the saddle and tried to jerk the bird up out of the hole. The cowboy who got the rooster was chased by the losing riders, who tried to grab the bird. If a *vaquero* managed to outride the grasping hands, he was permitted to bestow the rooster on the lady of his choice and keep the money that was buried in the hole the bird had occupied.

Santos Gamboa came through the crowd of spectators as the third rooster was being torn to pieces by *vaqueros* racing by on their horses. He tapped Jacinto on the shoulder. "I am going back to Agua Mansa. You stay with the gamecock. That will please Señora Gomez."

"*Gracias.*" Jacinto remembered his manners.

"I'll look after the boy," promised Joshua Dove, who was leaning against a tree trunk, looking disgusted by the bloody *corrida de gallos*. "Did you get your business done with Don Pedro and the priest?"

Gamboa smiled. "*Sí*, old Aldama says he will help us get a priest. He will write the bishop, and the little priest will speak to his superior, too. We even talked of the name of our parish. If the priest who comes agrees, we shall name it in honor of San Salvador."

Jacinto saw the riders converge again on the *vaquero*, who held the rooster aloft, challenging them. The bird was dead.

Joshua Dove said, "Not bein' a Catholic I wouldn't know about San Salvador."

"San Salvador is the Holy Savior, Don Joshua." Without another word Gamboa moved back through the crowd toward the corral. Jacinto looked after him and marked how even *caballeros* made way for the Indian.

"Santos Gamboa does not remain for the fight between the bear and the bull or to see El Cobarde?" Teodoro sounded astonished.

"He thinks only of corn and beans," muttered Jacinto.

The fight between the grizzly and the wild bull was held at four o'clock. Jacinto, so full of barbecued beef that his stomach hurt, found a place to stand with Teodoro between the seats of two pretty Mexican girls on top of the bullring.

Vaqueros held the bull steady with many ropes while others roped the bear and dragged him, bound and roaring, into the ring. Everyone looked on breathlessly while the *vaqueros* tied the right hind foot of the bear to the left front foot of the struggling, bellowing bull. Then swiftly the cowboys pulled off all other ropes and got out of the way of the two animals. Natural enemies on the range, the bear and bull began to fight at once. The bear rose to his full height and reached out with his horrible eight-inch-long claws to draw the bull to him at the same moment that the bull drove one of his horns into the bear. Deep bellowing and hoarse roaring drowned out the cries of the fascinated Californians. Foam and blood soon covered the struggling, swaying animals as the bear bit and clawed and the bull gored again and again. Less than five minutes of battle had passed before the bear fell dead, gored through a vital organ. And a minute or so later the bull, bleeding to death from a wound in his throat, collapsed, still tied to the corpse of the bear.

"*Bien hecho.* (Well done.) I've won a new comb!" cried the pretty girl nearest Jacinto. The Comanche boy could only shake his head, not at her behavior or her excitement at the strange contest but because the bull had been a fine young one and now was dead—wasted. Jacinto hoped Californians did not stage fights between their magnificent horses, too, and waste them the same way.

At dusk the two boys went back to Tío Carlos and found him dozing. They had learned from a *vaquero* that the cockfighting would take place in a small outbuilding behind the ranch house. The *vaquero* had added that no women would be present at the cock mains and the betting would be very heavy. Don Quirino would come with his sons and old Don Pedro, too. The head of the Aldama family preferred cockfighting to any other sport.

When it was almost dark, Jacinto took El Cobarde from his cage. While Teodoro and Tío Carlos were occupied with two of their novice cocks, the Comanche boy carried his rooster to a deserted place next to the corral and tied on the murderous knives that the blacksmith had made. Until then he had been carrying them in their protective leather scabbards. The spurs on El Cobarde, he put the scabbards back over the blades. Listening to a woman singing, accompanied by guitars, he pulled open the drawstring of Carmela Gomez's bag and shook the contents out into his hand. It felt like ground meat, but with a very sharp odor. Jacinto threw the food into the dust. El Cobarde went to it at once. By habit he pecked at it, threw up his head, and swallowed. Then as Jacinto watched, the bird began to tremble.

The boy put the sack back into his shirt, picked up El Cobarde, and walked with him to the outbuilding. While he waited for the Aldamas, Jacinto felt his bird quiver several times. And then suddenly El Cobarde fluttered in his arms and started to crow as the other young cocks did.

Then the Aldamas arrived with three of their Indian servants carrying gamecocks. Don Pedro sat in the only chair, one made of steer horns, with a red plush seat. El Chino took a bird, a speckled gray one, from a *vaquero* and stepped up onto a platform, which was well lit from below by many candle lanterns.

He looked around at the throng of men and boys, staring coolly at those who had birds. Suddenly he looked directly at Jacinto and called out, "You, the Indian from Agua Mansa, you with the white bird. What is his name?"

"Blanquito."

"Who trained him?"

"I did—and the Widow Gomez."

Everyone present laughed—Teodoro, too. Jacinto noticed in a fury that even Don Pedro's granite face split in a grin.

"Who would bet on such a bird?" called out El Chino.

"I'm doin' it," yelled Joshua Dove. "I'll bet a steer hide that Blanquito wins."

Men's voices rose at once in an uproar, taking part in the betting, wagering horses, mules, and cowhides.

Pushed by Teodoro, Jacinto stepped up onto the platform. He held El Cobarde head to head with El Chino's bird, pulled him back, then shoved him forward again. The gray rooster screamed in rage and tried to peck El Cobarde. Acting most unlike himself, El Cobarde reared in Jacinto's arms, pecking and screeching, too.

Jacinto pulled the scabbards off the long metal blades while El Chino did the same for the gray cock. At the very instant that El Chino threw his bird onto the platform, Jacinto flung El Cobarde down. There was no sound from the birds or from the many watchers except for the *whick-whick* of the cocks' wings. The neck feathers of both birds stood straight up as they circled each other. Suddenly El Cobarde exploded into a fury of white feathers. He leaped high into the air over the gray bird, raking downward with his spurs. He landed softly, but one blade was scarlet with the blood of El Chino's rooster.

The Comanche boy was open-mouthed with surprise. Señora Gomez had predicted that El Cobarde would have courage, and he was showing it. He flung himself headlong at the gray, meeting the other bird breast to breast, pecking savagely. El Cobarde leaped high once more, raking again, and this time bloodied the other blade.

As the Aldama bird collapsed onto the platform, a heap of bleeding feathers, Jacinto identified the smell of the food he'd given El Cobarde. It was gunpowder that the Widow Gomez had put into Blanquito's meat. That was the secret of his sudden courage.

El Chino did not pick up his dead bird. A *vaquero* hauled the body away while Jacinto carefully picked up the struggling, strutting El Cobarde and stepped down into the crowd.

Teodoro and Tío Carlos were open-mouthed as El Chino approached Jacinto. "Will you sell me that fine bird? Señor Dove tells me secretly that the husband of this Widow Gomez was a great trainer of game-cocks."

Jacinto shook his head. He'd noticed glances of admiration for the bird as he put the scabbards on to keep himself from being cut. He thought of how proud

Señora Gomez would be when she was told of the fight.
No, he could not sell Blanquito without her permission. Even more, though, he wanted to show off the fine
victorious bird in Agua Mansa!

"There will be cockfighting here two weeks from
Sunday. Bring your bird and we'll speak of this again.
I'll match him with my El Ladino."

Teodoro found his tongue to answer El Chino before Jacinto could. "I'll bring him here, El Chino.
He'll match his bird with El Ladino. Then Spotted
Wild Horse can tell you how his people, the Comanches, break horses."

El Chino was smiling as Tío Carlos got up onto the
platform to match one of the Ramirez novice cocks
against a second Aldama Bird. "Do you like horses?"
El Chino asked Jacinto.

"We Comanches call horses 'god-dogs,' " Jacinto replied gravely.

"And you have no horse of your own?"

"*Sí, patrón,* I have no horse—as yet."

"But you have a very fine bird. I would like to see
how he fares with El Ladino. Perhaps he will win a
horse for you."

El Chino stalked off to stand beside his grandfather's
chair and speak to the old man. As El Cobarde calmed
down in Jacinto's arms, the boy wondered about the
gamecock El Chino had mentioned twice to him. El
Ladino meant *outlaw.*

BY
THE
RIVER

VI

Joshua Dove and his wife didn't stay the full three days
of *fiesta*. They left on the afternoon of the second day,
and Jacinto and El Cobarde went with them, leaving
Tío Carlos and Teodoro behind to match their veteran
gamecocks with others.

The old Yankee was full of praise for El Cobarde
as they rode home over the plain so dry that the horses
and mules broke through its crust. "I won me a heap
on that there bird o' yours. You tell Señora Gomez that
she's some bird trainer."

"I will tell her, Don Joshua." Jacinto smiled, thinking of the fine time he'd had at the *fiesta*. He'd had
"fat cow" in plenty and had seen the *vaqueros* do things
he didn't really believe. He'd watched them gallop at

a full-grown steer, grab it by the tail, and flip it over onto its back. El Chino had been very gracious to him. He'd taken him with Teodoro to see the most famous horse in California, the one called Huechino. Don Quirino owned the horse and kept it in a special corral. It was an ordinary-looking brown animal, though its tail was curly. El Chino told Jacinto why this horse was so valuable. Huechino was the finest horse in all California for bear hunting. He was strong, quick moving, and without fear of the smell of bears. Privately Jacinto thought El Chino was exaggerating about the brown horse, but how could he tell? The grizzly in the bullring had been the only bear the Aldamas had at the moment. Huechino had helped capture him.

Teodoro had told Jacinto that perhaps someday he'd be lucky enough to see a *vaquero* deal with a bear out in open country. *Vaqueros* ranging near the mountains were always on the lookout for bears for Huechino to battle. Perhaps if the youngest of the Aldamas took a real liking to him, he and Teodoro would be invited to ride out on Aldama horses. Then they could hunt bears also. *Vaqueros* would go with them. It was the duty of a California cowboy to get rid of a prowling bear that would attack the calves and colts.

Sí, Jacinto decided he had much to look forward to on Rancho San Bernardino. He'd go to the Aldama rancho again and match El Cobarde with the Aldama cocks. He would try to make friends with El Chino and get to ride a fine California horse. Then after he'd fought Utes and hopefully seen a *vaquero* fight a bear, he'd take his pick of the horses from a herd and start for home.

The Widow Gomez was pleased that Blanquito had done so well in his first main. But to Jacinto's annoyance she seemed even more pleased that the head of the Aldama family was going to bestir himself to get the settlers' village a priest. Everyone had been so overjoyed to hear of Santos Gamboa's conversation with old Don Pedro that little attention was paid to Jacinto and El Cobarde. The important talk of Agua Mansa was of the church they were going to start building. It would be a small one, naturally of adobe, but a fine church all the same. Don Quirino had promised Gamboa at the *fiesta* that he'd send Indians to the mountains to cut down trees to be sawn into large planks for the roof. When the walls had been built, the timbers would be ready for the settlers.

An irritated Jacinto spoke to Carmela Gomez about the church the night he returned from the *fiesta*. "But what if no priest will come?"

She smiled and said, "There will be a priest, and very soon."

Jacinto turned his head away as he went on massaging El Cobarde. Apparently the old woman thought she could foretell the future. These Mexicans, Jacinto had decided long ago in Santa Fe, were very strange

people. They said that things were "going to happen,"
yet they weren't medicine men. Among the Comanches,
only the medicine men prophesied.

Because El Cobarde wasn't admired enough in Jacinto's estimation, the boy felt slighted. He was becoming very fond of the white rooster. Jacinto tried to make
up for the neglect of the settlers by talking to him in
his cage and caressing him when he came back from
herding. Let the people of Agua Mansa look forward
to their church. He and El Cobarde would look forward to another main. El Cobarde would become a
very famous bird, probably the most famous in California! All Jacinto and the cock needed from the
Widow Gomez was the meat and gunpowder. Let her
chatter with the other women about a priest. Let her
think she could look into the future!

To Jacinto's surprise, it seemed the old woman could
at that. Only ten days after the *fiesta* a stranger came
riding on a donkey one evening into Agua Mansa. He
was escorted by two Aldama *vaqueros* towering over
him on their horses. The stranger was a priest in a long
brown cassock and straw hat, and from the saddlebags
on the horses, he clearly meant to stay. The *vaqueros*
dismounted, removed the bags, took their hats off to
the priest, mounted again, and rode off in the galloping California style.

Jacinto watched Santos Gamboa go up to the priest.

With the other villagers the boy pushed forward to hear what was being said. Jacinto heard the priest tell Gamboa, "*Sí*, Don Pedro Aldama spoke to my superior, and I was sent to you because you asked for a priest. I am Padre Anton."

Anton? What kind of name was that, wondered Jacinto. It wasn't Spanish. And the priest didn't look like a Mexican. His hair was very short, but what could be seen of it under his hat was not black. And his eyes certainly weren't brown, though they weren't the blue of Joshua Dove's.

"You are not Mexican?" Gamboa asked.

The priest smiled. "No, do you find my Spanish so bad?"

Hipolito Gamboa spoke up next. "Are you a *gachupin*, padre?"

Padre Anton smiled again. "Am I a man with spurs? A man from Spain? No, I am a Swiss."

"What is that?" a settler asked.

"Switzerland is a land very far away from California. It has many lakes and very high mountains with snow on them all year long."

Santos Gamboa said, "Padre, we had expected a Mexican to come to us."

"But I am the one who was sent to you. I am sorry if you are disappointed because I am a gringo, a foreigner." Padre Anton had stopped smiling.

"We plan to build a church for you, the sort of adobe

church men make in New Mexico. It will not be a great church of stone," said Gamboa.

"I have never been in New Mexico, but I think I would like a church of adobe." The priest took off his hat as he looked around at the village. Everyone gasped. His hair was the color of straw, and he was a good deal younger than Jacinto had guessed.

Gamboa went on, "We had it in mind to name our parish and the church in honor of San Salvador."

Padre Anton nodded. "I think you have chosen well to name your parish for our Lord Jesus himself. Where shall I stay? Where is a corral for my donkey?"

Jacinto noticed that everyone was looking at Santos Gamboa. Were they going to welcome this strange gringo priest or not? Would Gamboa tell him to go back to San Diego and ask that a Mexican come?

After a long silence Gamboa said, "You will live with me until a house is built for you. We shall build it along with the church." Then Gamboa ordered his sons, "Take the padre's saddlebags to my house and his donkey to a corral."

"Where do you plan to build the church?" asked the priest.

"Come, I will show you. Beside the river."

Jacinto and the thunderstruck settlers watched Gamboa and the yellow-haired priest walk off together until Carmela Gomez went running after them, calling, "Padre, padre!"

The priest turned around. "*Sí?*"

"Will you celebrate Mass on Sunday?" she asked, after she'd made a bobbling curtsey to him.

"I plan to, *señora*. I have brought what I need with me."

Jacinto frowned as he left to go back to El Cobarde. Mass so soon? And without a church? Well, it mattered nothing to him. He was going to the Aldama rancho with the gamecock next Sunday. He doubted if Gamboa would try to stop him. If Jacinto didn't appear with El Cobarde, Don Quirino might be displeased, and no settler wanted to annoy the powerful *patrón*.

Teodoro came to the Gomez house the next Sunday. He told Jacinto that his grandfather had gone on to the Aldamas in a cart and had taken four cocks with him.

The widow Gomez hadn't taken much interest this time in Jacinto's going to the rancho or even in El Cobarde's welfare. All she could talk about was the coming of Padre Anton, who for all his strangeness and his being so young was a fine man. He was polite even to the children and women and more than willing to listen to any problem. What was more, his advice was wisdom itself. He was going to start to say Masses for her dead husband's soul at once, something she'd long wanted.

Because the eager Teodoro had arrived early, Jacinto wasn't ready. He hurried into his best shirt, caught up El Cobarde in his cage and left after grabbing a *tortilla* and piece of goat's milk cheese. This food he ate as he sat on the mule behind Teodoro, his legs dangling while he held onto the gamecock's cage.

Not until he was halfway to the Aldama ranch house did Jacinto realize he'd forgotten to ask the Widow Gomez for her specially prepared ground-meat-and-gunpowder concoction. He could get meat from someone at the ranch house, but what of the gunpowder? And how much powder would he need? He glanced down at the rooster. El Cobarde was looking at him out of glittering black eyes. Jacinto sighed. The bird was in good condition. Perhaps the cock remembered winning his first main. He had seemed to enjoy it. Perhaps that joy of fighting and winning would make him win this one, too. Perhaps the meat the Widow Gomez had given him to feed the bird had been only a sort of Mexican trick that helped a rooster in his first fight. Would a gamecock so large and fine as El Cobarde need trickery again? Jacinto decided that the bird would not.

He asked Teodoro as they rode into the Aldamas' corral, "Do you know the cock the Aldamas call El Ladino?"

"I have seen him. He is black."

"Has he fought many times?"

"I have seen him fight only one time."

The boys found El Chino with Tío Carlos and some *vaqueros*, all of them watching a cowboy show his skill with the *reata*. His length of rawhide was a full sixty feet. Jacinto already had heard from a boastful Teodoro that a very expert *vaquero* could throw with great accuracy for fifty feet. The most skilled of all could even throw backwards. They could catch a galloping wild horse by any part of his body and bring him to the ground.

Jacinto watched the cowboy tie the *reata* about his waist and wave to a *vaquero* on a horse off in the distance. Beside him stood a riderless horse. Suddenly both horses came running forward, the riderless one, a sorrel, being driven ahead by the man. As the sorrel neared the *vaquero*, the cowboy started spinning his rope in a circle. When the sorrel was abreast of him, he threw out the loop. It settled over the horse's right hind leg as he ran by and instantly jerked taut as the horse fell. Jacinto saw the *vaquero* fall, too, then watched him leap up, arch his back and lift his hands into the air, digging his heels into the dirt at the same moment. While the other *vaqueros* looked on, laughing, the sorrel fell once more.

Annoyed because he was nowhere as good a roper as the Californians, Jacinto said to Teodoro, "That is not so wonderful."

Teodoro scoffed. "That was only the *mangana de muerte* (the throw of death) with a *reata* about the waist. Sometimes a *vaquero* will tie the rope about his neck and catch a horse with his *reata*. If he does not do it correctly, he may lose his head. It has happened."

Jacinto shook his head. "It is only a trick," he told Teodoro. "It is a foolish thing to kill yourself like that. Comanche men die in battle proving their courage."

The other boy shrugged. "Mexicans die in battle, too, but they like games with a *reata*."

Jacinto asked, "Why don't they tie *reatas* about their necks now?"

"Because Don Quirino and Don Pedro do not approve. They will not let El Chino do it anymore."

El Chino, who wore a fine mustard-colored velveteen jacket today, came over to the boys now. He peeked into El Cobarde's cage and nodded. "So, you have brought him? It is well. What will you bet on him?"

Embarrassed, Jacinto said, "I have nothing to bet."

"No one in Agua Mansa has very much," explained Teodoro loyally. "Spotted Wild Horse brought his bird only to please you, El Chino."

The youngest of the Aldamas slapped Teodoro on the shoulder. "Only to please me? I know you better than that, little one. What do you want?"

"To have mounts to ride out to see your herds of wild horses. Will you take us?"

El Chino asked Jacinto, "Will Santos Gamboa, who

rules you, let you go? Or does he work you in the fields day and night?"

"I can go on Sundays. The rest of the time I herd the sheep and goats. I do not work in the fields at all," Jacinto told him hotly.

The young man laughed. "You didn't need to tell me. There is the smell of goats about both of you. I know Teodoro sleeps with a goat." He looked directly at Jacinto. "Do you?"

"I do not sleep with goats," the Comanche boy flared.

El Chino ignored his anger. He looked up at the cloudless blue sky and began to sing. "I will give you a kiss that will make you forget your sorrows very soon."

Irked by El Chino's indifference, Jacinto decided to give him a piece of news to get his attention. "A priest has come to Agua Mansa. The settlers are going to build a church for him. He is not a Mexican."

This information interested the young man for a moment. "A priest? What is he if he's not a Mexican?"

"He is from a land he calls Switzerland."

"Is it near Spain?"

"I do not know, but he speaks Spanish well enough."

"Then it must be part of Spain." Whistling the same song, El Chino strolled off toward the corral.

"Teodoro, do you think he'll take us riding someday to see the wild horses?" asked Jacinto.

"We will not know until he comes with horses some Sunday."

The mains were held in the same outbuilding that evening, but because the *fiesta* was over fewer men were present. Tonight all of them were Aldamas or their *vaqueros*.

By the very bright light of an autumn full moon Jacinto tied the blades to El Cobarde's legs, whispering to the bird to give him courage. He liked the cock very much, more than he'd admit to anyone. Who had ever heard of a Comanche liking birds? "Win for me," he told El Cobarde. "You do not need the foolish Mexican tricks of the Widow Gomez." By the time he'd finished winding the last thread around the spur stumps, he felt quite confident.

But his first sight of El Ladino made his heart fall. The bird El Chino held was very large and he was black indeed, so black there seemed to be purple in his feathers. He fluttered in the young man's arms, and it seemed to Jacinto that El Cobarde was more quiet than he'd been at his first main.

Then the roosters were thrown down onto the platform. El Ladino attacked at once in a great hop, springing over El Cobarde. When the white cock turned to meet his assault, the Aldama bird leaped at him from the front, his shining black legs curved to his breast, the glittering blades slanted cruelly downward. As they struck, Jacinto let out a groan. Then he saw the dark ropy blood flowing from El Cobarde's beak.

"A wound in the lungs!" Tío Carlos called out, coming to the platform.

Jacinto looked on unhappily while El Cobarde sank down and lay still, his eyes closed. The main had lasted only a few seconds. El Cobarde was dying. But old Tío Carlos didn't seem to think so. Calling out *"Carrio,"* he reached down and set El Cobarde on his feet. To Jacinto's great joy the white bird flurried toward the black one and leaped over El Ladino, slashing his left side as he passed over him.

"Tabla, tabla!" Tío Carlos shouted. "It is a draw. It is a tie. They have both drawn blood."

But El Chino didn't pick up his bird, and Jacinto was too bewildered by the sudden recovery of El Cobarde to grab him.

The Aldama bird flung himself into the air, a silent fury of glistening ebony feathers. One of his knives buried itself deep between El Cobarde's fluttering wings. Bound to each other by the terrible blade, the birds rolled as one off the platform. *Vaqueros* got out of their way quickly to give the gamecocks room and instantly formed a circle around them.

Standing on the platform's edge, Jacinto watched bright blood well out over El Cobarde's back and flow over the black bird's feet. Then El Cobarde fell, a pile of bloodstained feathers under the black cock.

El Chino jumped down and pulled his struggling bird off El Cobarde. He held the black cock high in the air, smiling widely. His gesture told all there was to tell. His bird had won. The bird from Agua Mansa was dead.

Finally a *vaquero* called out to Jacinto, "The Widow Gomez failed you this time. You should have sold the cock to El Chino."

Jacinto felt anger rising. Yes, she had failed him and El Cobarde. She was the cause of the cock's losing— she and the priest and the church. She should have given Jacinto another bag of meat and gunpowder, without his having to ask her for it.

"Go, boy, take the cock away. It is time for the next main," Tío Carlos told Jacinto. "It is the way in cockfighting."

Jacinto got down among the spectators. No one spoke to him as he picked up El Cobarde. All of the men were looking at El Ladino and at a magnificent red bird with green-black legs and golden neck feathers. Clearly El Ladino was to be matched with this new cock. Jacinto hoped the red bird would kill him. Clearly also El Ladino had fought many birds. Teodoro might have known this all along. His having said that he'd seen the black bird fight only once didn't mean anything. Teodoro could have been holding back information. After all, he didn't care about El Cobarde. He'd given him away.

Carrying his dead bird in his arms, Jacinto left the building. He wouldn't stay there, holding his bird, to watch the other mains. He would never go to another cockfight. It wasn't a thing Comanches did. In the moonlight El Cobarde's blood was black on the pale feathers and against Jacinto's white shirt. Let Señora Gomez see the blood and wash it out, if it would come out. She would certainly try. He was wearing the fine shirt she had made for him for the *fiesta*. He hoped it was ruined.

Jacinto walked toward the large corral. He stared wistfully at the horses, then went on, heading west toward the river past the Aldamas' irrigation canal. He'd had enough of Californians for a time. He hoped El Chino would come with horses someday soon. But even if the young man offered him a horse right now, Jacinto would refuse it. He felt tricked by the Aldamas and by Teodoro. Cockfighting was like the Mexican tricks played on horseback or with the *reata*. All foolish. These tricks could kill men and animals, too. Jacinto thought of the wild bull killed at the *fiesta*. It had been a valuable one who could have sired fine calves. No, he could not understand the Mexicans. He hadn't understood them in Santa Fe. They were even harder to understand in California.

The boy felt the bird growing cool in his arms as he walked toward Agua Mansa. He would greatly miss

El Cobarde. In a way the gamecock had become a pet,
something Jacinto had not had since childhood when
he'd played with grasshoppers and a fat yellow puppy
that resembled a young coyote. Servants in the houses
of powerful men in Santa Fe didn't own pets. Now,
vowed Jacinto, he would never have another pet.
Horses he would have, *sí*. But horses were not pets.
They could be greatly beloved and mourned when
they died, but they were more a form of wealth than
pets. They were valuable gifts a man gave to honor his
friends or to buy himself a bride.

Jacinto gazed down at the rooster. In a way the
cock had meant wealth, too, though neither Jacinto
nor anyone else from Agua Mansa had gained anything
from him—only Joshua Dove had profited. When you
had nothing to wager, how could you gain? But El
Cobarde had made Jacinto feel important. An animal
that could make money was more respected than one
who could not, and so was his owner.

Walking downhill, choosing the easiest way, Jacinto
went toward Agua Mansa. He kept an eye out for bulls
and bears until he came to the Santa Ana River a mile
or so north of the village. He placed the dead bird
under a tree and waded out into the stream to wash his
hands and to drink. As he drank he had a terrible
thought. El Cobarde had been a healthy young bird.
What was to prevent Señora Gomez from plucking and

cooking the rooster? Sometimes she had joked about how very fine he would taste because of the special diet she kept him on.

No, Jacinto told himself fiercely. That would not happen to his brave bird. Muttering in Comanche, he came out of the river and fell onto his knees under the tree. The earth was damp and soft where the tree sucked up moisture. He would bury El Cobarde there. The blood on his shirt would be enough to let the people of Agua Mansa know how things had fared at the Aldama rancho.

Jacinto began to dig into the earth with his knife. When he had the hole dug, he picked up El Cobarde and held him to his breast, speaking lovingly to him in Comanche. Then, bending low, Jacinto put El Cobarde into the hole.

Before he could push the dirt over the cock, he stiffened suddenly, listening. Then he lay down flat with his ear to the ground. Over the running of the river he heard something. The sound of hooves! Many horses or many cattle were approaching. Perhaps one of the wild bands coming to the river to drink. If what he heard was horses, he meant to see them. Above him was a tree with a fork just low enough for Jacinto to scramble up into. He climbed hurriedly into the cottonwood and sat astride a branch, for the hooves were coming very swiftly from the west.

Almost at once Jacinto saw them in the moonlight,

many horses coming toward the shallow stream, their manes and tails floating as they ran. After a moment the boy realized they weren't running free in the night. There were other horses at a distance behind them, horses with riders. Jacinto held tight to the branch with both hands, peering down as the driven horses splashed through the Santa Ana. And now the men came. They were not *vaqueros*. Not one of the dozen or so riders wore a hat as *vaqueros* always did.

Suddenly Jacinto knew as they passed beneath his tree. These men had long dark hair held out of their eyes by bands of cloth across their foreheads. They were Indians—Ute raiders! Jacinto remembered that Utes sometimes came with the full moon, though they had not appeared for over a year.

The raider who followed last stopped in the shallows of the Santa Ana to let his horse drink. The animal drank long enough for Jacinto to get a good look at the rider. This Indian wore a necklace of grizzly bear teeth, long and white, gleaming on his chest.

In his heart Jacinto felt sure that he was looking at the Ute chief, Walkara, who would be as much an enemy of his father, Big Wolf, as of Don Quirino Aldama or Santos Gamboa. Jacinto sucked in his breath, wishing he had his bow and arrows instead of only his knife.

The Utes were stealing California horses, and there was nothing he could do but remain quiet in his hiding place. Some of the raiders had muskets. He'd seen the white shine of the metal in the moonlight. The man who might be Walkara had a musket, too. A sling held it across his broad dark chest with its muzzle sticking up behind his shoulder. A Ute would be happy to kill a Comanche, armed or unarmed. For that matter a Ute would kill anyone he thought stood in his way.

Jacinto didn't move from his perch until the chief's horse had come up out of the river and passed out of sight behind a hill to the north. The raiders headed toward Cajon Pass.

After climbing down the tree, he buried El Cobarde, all the while thinking angrily about the raiders. He'd stayed in California for only two reasons—to get horses and to fight the Utes. And, of course, because the Aldamas *insisted*. The horses the Utes drove off had been good ones, horses any Comanche would have been proud to own. By stealing horses from the rancheros, the Utes stole from Jacinto, who wanted horses as badly as they did. And he hadn't struck one blow against them!

QUICKSAND

VII

Because Agua Mansa was nearer, Jacinto decided he'd go there to tell the news about the raiders. Santos Gamboa could send a rider on his white mare to alert the Aldamas.

The Comanche boy crossed the Santa Ana, then ran over a mile along its west bank until he reached the village. Out of breath, he came rushing into Gamboa's house without hailing anyone. Gamboa, his wife, and Hipolito sat on a bench before their small fireplace. Padre Anton, who had the only chair, was reading aloud from a small leather-bound book. When he saw Jacinto in the doorway, his eyes grew wider but he said nothing, only closed the book.

Santos Gamboa got up swiftly and grabbed the

musket standing in the corner near the chimney, then reached for his hat. He questioned Jacinto in rapid Comanche, "What is it? There is blood on you. Was it a bear? Where is the Ramirez boy?"

Jacinto shook his head and answered also in Comanche, "It is the Utes. They are driving off horses. The blood is El Cobarde's. He was killed, and I was bringing him away when I saw the raiders."

"Where did you see them?"

Jacinto told him quickly, watching Gamboa take up a bag of food kept ready and ammunition for the musket. When he'd finished, Gamboa nodded and spoke to his wife in Spanish. "Magdalena, go to the houses I have told you of before. Tell the men of each house that the Utes have come and driven off horses. Tell them to be in the plaza as quickly as possible."

Padre Anton got up as Señora Gamboa ran out of the house. "Santos, you have no horses! You cannot go after these Indians on foot."

"We will catch them in the mountains," Gamboa told the priest. "Not even horses can move swiftly there, and the Utes must make camp at some time."

"I think the chief was Walkara," Jacinto said.

"Why do you say that?" Gamboa halted at the door.

"I saw one raider who wore a necklace of grizzly bear teeth."

Gamboa nodded. "Sí, he would be a chief." Then he was gone.

The priest and Jacinto stood staring at each other. Finally the man said, "If we had a bell, we could get the settlers together more quickly. It would be a signal to them."

"If we had a bell, we'd have a church!" Jacinto's voice was sharp with anger. In a way this man, too, had been the cause of El Cobarde's death.

"You don't want a church?" asked Padre Anton, sounding surprised.

"Why should I care? I am not a Genizaro. I'm a Comanche, the son of Big Wolf of the Honey Eaters. He is a chief."

The priest sighed. "You do not want to help build a church?"

"No. I didn't want to come to California. I was sent here by my *patrón* in Santa Fe."

"Then you will not have to help. I'll ask Santos to see that you do not have to work on it."

"*Gracias*, that would please me." Jacinto started out of the Gamboa house but stopped at the door when the priest called out after him.

"Whose blood is on your shirt?"

"My bird, El Cobarde. He was very brave."

"Ah," said Padre Anton. "Cockfighting." He shook his head.

Jacinto smiled at the priest. "*Sí*, cockfighting on Sunday. There is often cockfighting on Sundays at the Aldama rancho, and much gambling."

"But not in Agua Mansa, I hope." The priest was frowning.

The boy scoffed, "No, not in Agua Mansa. Who would gamble here? I had the only gamecock in the village."

The priest's frown had been replaced by a look of melancholy. "Will you want another bird?"

"No, not another," Jacinto replied.

"I am very pleased to hear it. What is your name?"

"Spotted Wild Horse is my Comanche name. They call me Jacinto here, but I didn't choose that name."

"Would you like me to call you Spotted Wild Horse?"

Jacinto shrugged. "Call me what you will."

"Then you will be Spotted Wild Horse."

The boy went out into the plaza and walked through the throng of men assembling to chase the Utes. He looked on as one of Gamboa's sons rode the white mare out of the village to the Aldama rancho with the message.

"*Vaqueros* will join us," Gamboa said to his New Mexicans. He waved his arm, and the men started out at a trot behind him. The moon was so bright they had no need of lanterns.

When they were gone, Jacinto strolled by the somber-faced women to the Widow Gomez's house. Like many of the other women, she'd stood in the doorway to see the men go. From the expression on her face he knew she was worried about them, too, though she had no man to lose anymore. He was pleased to hear her sudden gasp of horror when she caught sight of the stain on his shirt.

"*Ay de mí,*" she cried. "You were wounded by the Utes!"

Jacinto went past her. "The blood is El Cobarde's."

"Thanks be to San Isidro that you are not harmed."

"Old woman, El Cobarde is dead. He was killed by the Aldama cock. It is your fault."

"My fault?" Her mouth fell open. She closed the door and leaned against it.

"*Sí,* you thought only of priests and churches. You did not give me the meat for El Cobarde before he must fight."

"*Ay de mí,* Jacinto, I forgot." The old woman pressed her hand to her forehead.

"And so the cock is dead," Jacinto told her bitterly. "I have buried him to keep him out of your pot."

Her eyes filled with tears. "I am sorry, Jacinto. I would not have cooked him. You are a good boy. You should have reminded me about the meat."

"You were interested in El Cobarde once. I almost thought we owned him together."

She reached out her arm for her *rebozo,* hanging on a peg near the door.

Jacinto said, "The priest is at Santos Gamboa's house, but you'd better not go to him to tell him your

troubles. I told him about El Cobarde and the cockfights at the Aldama rancho. I didn't tell him *you*
trained the bird. He didn't seem pleased that the men
of Agua Mansa were interested in cockfighting."

Her arm fell. She looked thoughtful. "Are you
hungry, Jacinto?"

"*Sí*, I am hungry."

"I will feed you, and then I will soak your shirt
overnight and wash it in the morning."

"As you please." Jacinto slipped his shirt off over
his head and handed it to her as she gave him his other
shirt.

"Thank you for not telling Padre Anton that I
trained gamecocks," she said. Then she asked, "Will
Teodoro give you another bird?" Before Jacinto could
answer she started ladling beans from her chili pot
onto a plate.

Jacinto said, "I will not have a bird if he offers me
one. With the priest here, Santas Gamboa would not
let me keep him, would he?"

The old woman looked up, suddenly hopeful. "You
could keep it secretly down by the river."

Jacinto was scornful. "Cocks crow. Gamecocks crow
even more loudly. I don't think the priest is a fool."

While she went outside to put his shirt in a pail of
water, Jacinto sat cross-legged on the floor, eating. He
stared absently into the corner where El Cobarde's
cage had stood. And suddenly he couldn't eat anymore.

He put his plate down on the dirt floor. When Señora Gomez returned he saw her glance in the same direction and hastily wipe her eyes on the hem of her red flannel petticoat.

"The blacksmith's dog has puppies," she said.

Jacinto thought about this news. "A dog would be good for you to have when I am not here."

"They will not grow to be large dogs."

"You don't need a large dog, *señora*. A dog who barks will be enough in the village. A cock is a good companion and watcher, but not so good as a dog."

The woman picked up Jacinto's dish and sat down on her stool, holding the plate on her knees. "Tell me of the Utes. I heard Gamboa saying to the men that you had seen them. He said you thought you had seen Walkara, their chief."

Jacinto told her about his experience. Then without being asked he spoke of the cockfight and of El Cobarde's defeat. He wasn't angry with her anymore.

When he finished, she let out a deep sighing breath. "So? You think this outlaw bird, this black El Ladino, was an experienced fighter? And your friend Teodoro might have known it?"

"I don't know, *señora*."

"Very likely you will never know. That is the way of cockfighting. There is little friendship when it comes to the losing and winning of property. Do you think El Chino will ever bring a horse here for you to ride?"

"Who knows? I do not understand him." Again Jacinto looked at El Cobarde's corner of the room. "I don't want to see El Chino for a while. I don't like Mexican tricks. The Aldamas know many of them."

"El Chino may not come. He and his family have lost many horses to the Utes now."

Jacinto smiled. "They still have more than they can count. They are very rich in horses. Someday I would like to have more horses than I could count."

The old woman spoke softly. "Jacinto, can you count? Padre Anton said after Mass today that he would like to have a school here in the village. He said that men who will someday be important in this new land must read and count well, so no one can ever cheat them."

Jacinto closed his ears as he'd done a hundred times before to her chattering. He didn't have to help build the church and he'd find some way to get out of going to Padre Anton's school. He could count to thirty on his fingers. And if he forgot how to count in the Spanish way, a Comanche could always carve notches on a stick to show how rich he was in horses. He'd go on herding animals until he fought Utes himself. Then he'd take his pick of the horses and leave California. He had a score to settle with El Chino and for that matter with all of the Aldamas for the death of El Cobarde. Taking their horses would be his payment.

*   *   *

The trackers came back to Agua Mansa five days later. They'd found the Utes camped in the desert some distance from Cajon Pass, but they hadn't been able to surprise them. The Utes had set out guards around their camp. Clearly the raiders knew Gamboa and his people had come to the valley. One of the *vaqueros* said that the Utes probably had sent out scouts before they came raiding this time. The New Mexicans and Aldama cowboys had killed four raiders and recovered twenty horses, but there had been losses, too. A *vaquero* had been killed by a raider's gun, and Hipolito Gamboa's handsome face was marred for all time. He had been struck in the right cheek by an arrow that smashed bones and teeth. Fortunately, the arrow missed his eye. Still, everyone was pleased that at last the New Mexicans had proven their worth to the Aldama family, who had given them land.

The settlers rested for a few days, then started the process of making adobes again. It was late autumn, the season of the "devil winds." The harvest had been gathered. Green chili peppers weathered to bright scarlet on the sides of the houses just as they did in New Mexico. Except for the hunting of antelope and deer, the men could give all their time to building the church. And when that was finished, they would build a house for the priest.

Jacinto herded the settlers' animals near the Santa Ana and tried not to think of El Cobarde or what might have been betrayal on Teodoro's part. Teodoro had not visited him at Agua Mansa since the night the Utes raided. In a way Jacinto was glad that he hadn't come. In another way he was annoyed. It would have been pleasant to see Teodoro's excitement while he listened to the story of the Ute raiders and heard Jacinto's description of the man who might be Walkara. Even El Chino would be interested, but he never came to Agua Mansa.

Each night at dusk when he returned with the flocks, Jacinto went to the riverbank to see how the church progressed. The walls rose swiftly because more than thirty men worked making cement and adobes and laying the large blocks on top of one another. Don Quirino, true to his word, had sent large beams sawn from mountain timbers.

Although the church was roofless, Padre Anton celebrated Mass in it twice a day. Six o'clock was the hour of morning Mass. Jacinto was careful to get the goats and sheep out of their corrals and on their way upstream or downstream before that hour. Escaping evening Mass was not so simple. Señora Gomez understood why he left so early with the flocks but was determined that he go to Mass with her after supper. Finally he asked her to speak to the priest about him. He guessed that if Padre Anton didn't want to force him to help build the church, he wouldn't mind if he didn't go to Mass.

The Widow Gomez returned in a fury from her conference with the priest. "I do not understand you," she railed at Jacinto. "Padre Anton says you may come when you are ready or when Don Santos says you must come. Then the priest will be happy to have you. You are very wicked, Jacinto."

"I'm not a Genizaro," he told her. "You've always known that. I'm a Comanche. Padre Anton knows it, too. I told him."

"Santos Gamboa is also a Comanche!"

"No, he is a Genizaro! He is no longer a Comanche."

The woman flared at him. "I told Padre Anton that I planned to talk to Señor Gamboa about your going to Mass."

Jacinto was alarmed. "What did the priest say?"

"That he had told Gamboa you need not come to Mass until you were ready."

Jacinto smiled. Padre Anton was a fair man. He only hoped that he would be as fair-minded about going to school.

By the first week of December the church was finished except for the roof, which had yet to be thatched and tarred. The New Mexicans had worked very hard and as swiftly as they could because again they feared the coming of January rains. Certainly they would have the church roofed by then to keep the adobes from melting.

Jacinto passed by it at dawn one cool morning driving his sheep and goats ahead of him. He gave it an unfriendly glance, thinking of the school that was to come to Agua Mansa, too. He decided that the church, compared to the churches of Santa Fe, wasn't a very fine one. He knew there was little inside it—no statues or pews—only a makeshift altar table set up on the dirt floor with some cheap metal vessels and candlesticks on it. For all the talk about a bell, there wasn't even a belfry or bell tower. The farmers of Agua Mansa probably didn't know how to build one. Jacinto was hastening past the nearly finished building, eager to get out of sight of the coming worshippers, when two of his goats began to fight. Hitting the larger one on the back with his shepherd's stick to drive him off, the boy grabbed the other by his beard.

While he was tugging at the goat, Jacinto suddenly felt a shivering under his feet. He looked down and saw a ripple of movement. Terrified, he let the goat go. It ran off bleating its fear, and at once the rest of the flock bolted after it. Again the earth shuddered.

Jacinto fell to his knees, feeling another shudder. And now he heard the sound, an awful cracking and crunching noise that came from the church. The boy looked up in terror at the front of the building. What he saw made him cry out in fright. He scuttled on all fours backwards, pushed himself up by his hands, spun about, and ran. He stopped twenty feet from the church, his arms flung up over his head, eyes fixed in disbelief on the building.

It was swaying. Then it was falling. The walls collapsed outward toward him while the heavy timbers that served as the crossbeams of the side walls fell into the interior of the church.

Jacinto turned and ran again until the noise had stopped and the earth ceased to shiver. Then he stared.

The new church was gone. Only a pile of crumbled adobes and timbers sticking out of the ruined shell remained where the church had stood.

If Jacinto had stayed on his knees, the front of the church would have fallen on him, crushing him under tons of adobe bricks. He stood dazed and unbelieving that such a thing could have happened, as the settlers on their way to Mass ran up to him, followed by the ashen-faced priest.

"What has happened?" Jacinto heard Padre Anton ask Santos Gamboa. Gamboa was the first to reach the ruined building, and he stood nearest the collapsed front wall.

"Did the earth move?" shouted a New Mexican who had made cement for the adobes.

Gamboa didn't answer the questions. Jacinto watched him walk around the ruins, climb over a fallen wall, and look inside. Then he gazed at the village and finally at the river.

"Our houses are not damaged. It was not an earthquake," Gamboa frowned and sighed. "It must be as Don Joshua said to me once. It is God's will."

"It is God's mercy all of us were not inside hearing Mass," said Padre Anton. He stood quietly, his eyes on the collapsed church. "We would have been crushed to death. What did Don Joshua tell you?"

"It is the fault of the river."

"The river?" asked the priest.

"*Sí.* Don Joshua told me that we were not wise to build here, but I didn't listen to him. The Santa Ana runs in a new bed these days. Don Joshua said this is the old riverbed, if you believe the words of the Indians who lived here when he first came to California. He said this land is made of sand but under it lies water, much water underground. Our church was too heavy for the layer of sand under it."

"We built on quicksand then," exclaimed Padre Anton.

Quicksand! Jacinto remembered now that Teodoro had spoken to him about the Santa Ana having quicksands in it. Once long ago a cartload of padres on their way to the *asistencia* from Mission San Gabriel had been caught in quicksand. They had not dared to move from their cart for fear it might be engulfed. Two Indian drivers had got out of the cart to keep the heads of the oxen out of the sand and water, while a priest on each side of the cart held on tight to an Indian's long hair. The padres, oxen, and Indians held their positions all day long until a passing Indian was hailed and sent running to the *asistencia* for help. Jacinto and Teodoro had laughed, picturing the priests grabbing Indians by the hair.

His heart still beating rapidly from his escape, Jacinto was suddenly giddy. All he could do was laugh in spite of himself, thinking of the amusing picture of the priests and Indians. Then he became aware that everyone was glaring at him, and the laughter stopped in his throat. People's eyes were agatelike with anger. Gamboa's were slits of glittering darkness. The man jumped forward, grabbed Jacinto by the shoulders, and started to shake him. Bellowing, Gamboa told him he was sorry he'd ever brought him to California. He was a disgrace to the village and must have his hair cut at once. It was too long. He was not a Genizaro, but he was not to act like a Comanche either. Gamboa shook him again, still shouting. "Now you *will* go to Mass and you *will* help build our new church after you bring the animals back here each evening. Go, gather the flocks, and be on your way. Be thankful I don't whip you out of the village and leave you to the bears and bulls."

"*Sí*, leave me to them!" Jacinto shouted in Comanche, hauling at the bow slung across his chest.

"No, no!" Padre Anton saw the gesture and raised his hands. "The boy meant no harm. He was in great danger from the fall of the church. He did not mean to laugh."

Gamboa turned to face the priest. "He is not sorry that the church has fallen, our work on the walls wasted, and the altar crushed by a beam. You heard this boy laugh, padre."

"I don't want hate between you and him," said the priest softly.

"There has been bad blood between us ever since we took his knife from him on the trail from Santa Fe. He didn't want to come to California. I knew what was in his heart."

Padre Anton had his back to the ruined building. "Spotted Wild Horse, if you didn't want to come here, why did you?"

"I told you once before. I was sent here." Jacinto pointed angrily at Gamboa. "He forced me to come. Don Quirino Aldama forces me to stay here because he needs people on his rancho. But that's not why I stay—not because of them. I want to fight Utes. All Comanches hate Utes."

"That is all you want?"

Jacinto lied. "That is all. If I kill a Ute, I will be a Comanche man."

The priest shook his head. "Taking pride in killing men, even if they are heathen Indians, is an evil thing."

Gamboa spoke before Jacinto could. "Killing Utes is necessary, padre. Do not forget it is our bargain with the Aldamas. We must fight the raiders or lose our land. There are too many people in New Mexico for what little good farmland there is. We cannot go back."

Padre Anton breathed deeply but said nothing. Folding his hands behind his back, he started to walk around the church. After a moment Gamboa and the other men followed him. Jacinto heard Gamboa call out as he pointed below the bluff behind the village. "We will build the new church there on higher ground, padre. We can use the timbers that haven't broken and some of these same adobes. We'll start at once, but in the meantime couldn't you say Mass in a ramada again?"

"*Sí*," the priest replied. "As soon as you think it's safe I'd like to go inside and see if I can salvage anything of the church vessels. If I can't, a man will have to ride to San Diego for me with a message to my bishop to send new vessels."

By now Jacinto's face had stopped burning with anger. His bold words to Padre Anton had made him feel less embarrassed, had almost blotted out Gamboa's public scolding and shaking. He picked up his stick and looked around him for the goats and sheep. He couldn't help seeing how the settlers glared at him. They weren't weeping over the ruined church anymore. One woman, who was half-Mexican, muttered, "The Comanche boy put a curse on our church." She crossed herself. "That is why it fell down. See his hair. It is like a girl's."

"Don Santos should beat you with that stick you have," said a man, as Jacinto passed him.

And a young woman added, "You brought that gamecock into the village and went to cockfights on a Sunday. You brought ill fortune to us."

"And you will bring more wherever you go," said another woman, one with a baby in the folds of her *rebozo*.

The Widow Gomez waited some distance away, holding a half-grown ewe sheep by the neck, until he came up to her. "The church was begun on a Tuesday," she told Jacinto, as he took the ewe. "All Mexicans know anything begun on a Tuesday will go very badly." She whispered so no one else could hear. "Jacinto, I am happy that you will go to church from now on. You won't be going to the rancho with the Ramirez boy anymore. Teodoro was not good company for you. I will cut your hair for you tonight."

"Teodoro is my only friend here," Jacinto told her coldly, pushing the ewe in front of him with his stick.

"Padre Anton is your good friend. Jacinto, he saved you from the anger of Don Santos."

"Don" Santos? Gamboa had been called that by the New Mexicans only recently. Jacinto hurried off in pursuit of a strayed goat he saw in the distance. No, he had no intention of giving up Teodoro, though he'd

never accept another gamecock from him. Not even if
it was the very bravest of the Ramirez birds! He'd
visit Teodoro soon. There was good grazing in the
direction of the Ramirez house. He'd take the flocks
there just as soon as the rain started and the grass grew
more moist and green.

Teodoro and Tío Carlos wouldn't think that he'd
caused the collapse of the church. They'd know about
the river's quicksand and consider Gamboa a fool not
to have listened to Joshua Dove. They wouldn't say
that Jacinto had brought bad luck. And Teodoro
would understand how it hurt his pride to have his
hair cut short. Teodoro knew that Jacinto had hoped
to wear Comanche braids as soon as his hair was long
enough.

BLACK
HOOF

VIII

As soon as he could Jacinto drove his animals to the
Ramirez house. Both Teodoro and his grandfather
came outside to admire the sheep and goats. Five ewes
and one ram had survived the cruel journey from
New Mexico. Since the settlers' arrival the number of
sheep had grown to ten. The old Mexican praised the
strong chests of the sheep and the silky hides of the
goats, saying that the breeds of wool-bearing animals
from mountain country were often superior to California animals. Jacinto didn't tell him the goats had
been donated by Don Quirino.

Teodoro walked with Jacinto while he watched the
grazing animals. He told Jacinto that El Chino's black
rooster had killed two of the Ramirez birds that same

night, and the red one, too. "Our birds were not novice
cocks," he added, sighing.

Hearing this news made Jacinto feel better. Perhaps
Teodoro hadn't known what a very skilled fighter El
Ladino was. "El Chino likes to have his birds win,"
Jacinto said calmly. "He has many birds and many
horses. The Aldamas are rich."

"That's true," Teodoro agreed. "They don't know
what one bird or one mule or one horse means to a
poor man. You went away very quickly that night,
Spotted Wild Horse."

"I wouldn't leave El Cobarde there. I buried him."
Jacinto's voice was proud. "Because I did that, I saw
the Utes. I saw a chief who might be Walkara so near
me that I could have put an arrow through him if I'd
had my bow with me."

"*You* saw the Utes! I had heard they raided, but
no one said *you* saw them."

Jacinto relished his time of glory. "*Sí*, I gave the
alarm to Santos Gamboa, and he sent a rider to the
rancho." He told Teodoro how he'd watched the
raiders cross the Santa Ana.

"Mother of God, I would have been afraid."

Jacinto lied. "I was not. Comanches and Utes are
great enemies. I hope to see this chief again and next
time I'll be armed."

They talked of Walkara and the Utes and mourned
the loss of the fine horses they'd stolen. Then Jacinto

asked, "Has El Chino come here bringing a horse for you so you can ride out to see the herds?"

Teodoro's head dropped. "No, he hasn't come. I don't think he will. A *vaquero* came by here yesterday. He was laughing when he told Tío Carlos the news of El Chino."

"Why was he laughing?"

"El Chino stays around the house now. His sister has come home from a convent school in Chile and has brought a friend with her. She stays and stays—this friend. El Chino rides about with this girl sitting in his saddle. He sits behind on the horse's crupper, holding her about the waist. The *vaquero* says El Chino has eyes only for her, and there is talk that he wants to marry her."

Jacinto snorted. "Teodoro, he promised to come!"

"Tío Carlos said he thinks El Chino must be in love to give a girl the place of honor on his horse. He says that love makes young men crazy. They forget every promise they ever made."

"It won't happen to me," vowed Jacinto.

"I *hope* it doesn't to me," added Teodoro.

Jacinto sat down on a convenient rock, frowning. No horses! El Chino had failed them. He'd been a fool to trust him. And a worse fool to deliver El Cobarde up to the black cock. More Mexican trickery.

"Teodoro," he said suddenly, "we could borrow

horses from the herds of the Aldamas and no one
would ever know, couldn't we?"

Teodoro squatted in the shade of a cottonwood.
"The horses are wild."

Jacinto shrugged. "I know the Comanche way to
break a horse. We don't need saddles or bridles if we
ride like Comanches."

Teodoro's face twisted with thought. "I'm not a
Comanche. I need a saddle. We have spare bridles and
halters and one saddle. They're old but can be
mended." He looked at Jacinto. "What would the
Aldamas say if we borrowed horses?"

"They would never know that two horses had been
borrowed and broken." Jacinto knew in his heart that
he wasn't surprised at El Chino's failing them. If he was
ever to get a riding horse to take him back over the
Spanish Trail, he'd have to break one from the herd.
Others he could trail behind him, tied together. It
wouldn't matter if they were wild. No, it really
wouldn't be borrowing. It would be stealing, in fact.
And *vaqueros* dragged a man to death for stealing
horses! But no California *vaquero* had dealt with a
clever Comanche yet. On the other hand, Teodoro
wouldn't be stealing. If he wanted to he could return
his horse to the herd when Jacinto left. A horse broken
to the saddle and reins could be turned loose and run
with the wild ones again, and who would ever know?

"You'll use the *reata*, Teodoro," Jacinto ordered. "We'll break the horses together. And you'll hide them somewhere so we can go riding whenever we want."

Teodoro looked thoughtful and doubtful at the same time. "I know places to hide horses. But what if some Aldama *vaquero* sees us?"

"We won't go riding during the day. We'll ride at night." He gestured toward the flocks. "I have to be a shepherd every day but Sunday. And before it grows dark I have other work to do in Agua Mansa."

"For Señora Gomez?"

Jacinto sniffed. "Not for her. For the church. Remember there's a priest in Agua Mansa now." He told Teodoro about the collapse of the church and of Gamboa's order that he have his long hair cut at once and that he work on the church. "It was only because I thought of the story you told of the padres and the Indians stuck in the quicksand and it made me laugh that Gamboa got angry. Do you think I bring bad luck, too?"

"No," Teodoro scoffed. He was quiet for a while, playing with a twig broken from a tumbleweed bush. "I know why you wanted to grow your hair long. *Sí*, we will borrow horses. El Chino really meant to bring them to us. And I'm sorry that I got you to take El Cobarde to the rancho. If I rope horses for us, I'll feel better for having lost you the bird. You liked El Cobarde, didn't you?"

Jacinto nodded. "The Widow Gomez and I try not to look at the corner where his cage was kept."

"I'll give you another bird."

"No." The Comanche boy shook his head. "With Padre Anton in the village no one dares to have a gamecock. He doesn't like cockfighting at any time and especially on Sunday."

"But how will you get away from Señora Gomez so you can go riding with me?"

"She sleeps like a stone at night. She says she never rests, but she snores all night. If you can hide the horses halfway between here and Agua Mansa, we can ride out and I'll be back long before she wakes up. And if she should find that I'm gone, I'll tell her that I heard a noise out by the animals' corral and went to see what it was. Do you know a good hiding place that we could use?"

Teodoro's thin face lit up. "I know a little canyon in the hills where there's a small spring and grass. No one ever goes there because it's so small. When would you want to get horses?"

"When the next bright moon comes. Just before the next three-quarters moon, ride your mule out and look for the closest herd to the Santa Ana. Then watch the herd to see where it moves."

"You want a herd near the river?"

"We need the river and trees, Teodoro."

"But Tío Carlos says the river is treacherous," Teodoro objected. "Gamboa and the priest learned that when they built on quicksand."

"We're getting horses to ride for a while—not building churches we don't want. I want water—not sand." Jacinto smiled. "Did you know that Comanche boys our age go out together at night and take horses from men's bands and ride them without anyone in the tribe knowing about it?"

"Doesn't anybody ever find out? Do they bring the horses back?"

"Of course they bring them back." Jacinto reflected for a time. "Perhaps their fathers know. All Comanches do this when they're almost men like us. Then when they're war chiefs they boast about it in council."

"Mexicans would say that was stealing horses," said Teodoro.

Jacinto got up. "You aren't stealing, Teodoro. You're borrowing. The Aldamas owe you something, don't they?"

"Why do they?"

"Because El Chino and his father tricked you. El Ladino had won many cockfights. He'd fought more mains than your birds."

"*Sí.*"

"Then why shouldn't you ride one of their horses sometimes? You aren't taking it somewhere to sell it. That *would* be stealing."

Teodoro got up from under the tree. "I'll ride our

mule out to find the nearest herd, as you say. Then, I'll come see you."

Jacinto was scowling as he shouted at a goat trying to butt heads with another goat. "You'll probably find me making adobes," he told Teodoro, after he'd separated the goats.

For the remainder of that month Jacinto made adobes and cement for the church. He was polite to the Widow Gomez, Santos Gamboa, and the priest. The last thing in the world he wanted was for people in the village to start watching him more closely. If he made more trouble, he might be moved into the house of some settler who slept less soundly than Señora Gomez. It was easy to be pleasant now that Jacinto had his secret with Teodoro. Talking Teodoro into riding the horses would pay back El Chino, though he would never know.

The walls of the second church didn't rise as quickly as those of the first one. Adobe bricks made beside the Santa Ana had to be carried to the higher ground at the base of the western bluff. Gamboa had not ordered that Agua Mansa be moved also. If the houses of the New Mexicans also had been built on quicksand, they would surely have collapsed by this time.

When the moon reached three-quarters, Teodoro came on his mule to Agua Mansa. He walked around with Jacinto, looking at the fields being made ready for planting, pretending he was interested in them. But they walked together only to be out of earshot of the villagers.

"I looked for horses for five days," Teodoro told Jacinto. "There's a herd grazing beyond that great hill of rock west of here. I don't know if it will be there tomorrow. You know how horses move about. Anything from thunder to a little whirlwind of dust can start them running."

"Don't go far from here when you leave tonight. You'll have supper with Señora Gomez and me. When she's asleep, I'll come out to meet you. We'll scout the herd together. You have *reatas*?"

Teodoro grinned. "*Sí*. I have brought two strong ones. Why don't you take Gamboa's white mare so you will be riding, too?"

Jacinto shook his head. No, he wouldn't take the bell mare. Gamboa valued her. Sometimes he walked around the village at night as a Comanche walked, in silence, not stomping like a Mexican. Jacinto, watching from the window of the Gomez house, had seen him twice, his forehead wrinkled with thought as though he was worried. When Jacinto left the village and returned at night, he would have to be wary of Gamboa, who didn't sleep like the others, though he worked hard in the fields and on the church.

During supper, Teodoro behaved very well, saying all the Mexican polite things to Señora Gomez. He even asked her if she would accept a gamecock from him and train it. She refused, though Jacinto could see she was flattered. No, Padre Anton didn't approve of cockfighting, but he wouldn't know if she gave her recipe for meat mixed with gunpowder to Teodoro to pass on to Tío Carlos. This mixture might put great courage into some Ramirez cock and make him defeat the wicked black bird of the Aldamas. No one spoke of El Cobarde.

When Teodoro had gone, Jacinto waited until the old woman was asleep. Then he crept out of his blankets, took a rope of braided horsehair from the wall, and squeezed himself through the cowhide shutters at the back window. He ran to the rocks that rose out of the plain like mangled fingers and found Teodoro waiting on the mule. Jacinto heaved himself onto its back, and they set off at a trot toward the big rocky hill that blocked the way west. The distance wasn't far. If only the herd was still there!

To the great happiness of both boys, there were horses beyond the hill across the river. As Jacinto sat behind Teodoro looking down from a ridge on the side of the hill, he saw that the herd was not a large one but it was made up of good animals.

"What shall we do?" asked Teodoro softly.

Jacinto gazed at the countryside. The Santa Ana flowed beyond the hill, its banks bordered by trees. Finding the horses so near the water was more good luck. He pointed. "Take both *reatas* and climb one of the sycamores beside the river. I'll drive the horses under it, and you catch two as they run by."

Teodoro protested, "I can't catch two at once!"

"I know that. I'll drive them past the tree two times."

"What kind of horse do you want?"

"Comanches like pintos best."

"I'll try to get a pinto for you if I can."

They rode down to the riverbank where Teodoro slid off the mule and climbed the tree Jacinto picked out for him on the east side of the Santa Ana. A steep and slippery bank that rose up out of the water below the tree would slow down the horses as they came by.

Jacinto felt almost like a Comanche brave alone on the mule, which he quickly equipped with his horsehair rope. He didn't hurry to the herd. First he rubbed himself and his clothing with wild mustard to cover his own scent. When he guessed the distance from the wild horses was right, he slipped down by the mule's side, riding with his elbow in a sling of horsehair rope and the weight of his body on the middle of his upper arm. His heel hung across the back of the mule. When Jacinto wanted to rise up, he dropped his heel lower on the other side and pulled himself up. He hadn't ridden in this manner since childhood, but it wasn't any more difficult for him now than it had been then. In fact, it was easier because his arms and legs were stronger.

Guided by Jacinto, the Ramirez mule, which was accustomed to all sorts of antics from Teodoro, approached the herd. No horses became alarmed; they saw nothing but a riderless mule because Jacinto kept the mule's body between the herd and himself. Suddenly, when he was almost into the herd of wild horses, Jacinto pulled himself up by his heel. The horses were facing the right direction.

Jacinto yelled. The herd came alive at once. Startled, the horses began to canter, then gallop. They ran in a body, heading for the Santa Ana, snorting, hooves thudding. Jacinto yelled again, pounding after them, trying to move as swiftly as they did. But the pace was too much for the old mule. The boy lagged far behind, and by the time he was across the river the horses were out of sight. Jacinto was quite sure they'd passed under Teodoro's tree, which stood beside a narrow gap among the trees. He could only trust in Teodoro's alertness and skill with the *reata*.

What he saw under the sycamore astonished him. Not one but two horses were standing with *reatas* about their necks. One was a pinto, brown and white, Jacinto guessed, and the other a little white horse gleaming in the moonlight. What sort of Mexican trickery was this? *Two* horses?

Jacinto stopped the mule. "Teodoro," he called.

"Tie the mule and climb up here with me," came the voice from among the branches.

Jacinto tethered the mule to another tree and climbed the sycamore, dodging the teeth and hooves of the wild horses, which tried to attack him. He found his friend sitting in the crotch of the tree, grinning. The ends of the *reatas* were tied around stout limbs.

"Did you catch two *at once?*" Jacinto marveled.

"Not even a California *vaquero* can do that!" replied Teodoro delightedly. "No, the pinto came by in the front of the herd, so I dropped my *reata* over his head and looped it over the limb before he could jerk me out of the tree. Then I tied him fast. The small white horse was the last one over the river. I think she is a mare. She stumbled in the water. I saw her fall. I was ready with the second *reata* when she came underneath, but I missed her head. Then she came back."

"What?"

"*Sí,* the white one came running back. There may be a puma downriver. So I roped her, too, and tied her up with the pinto."

"You are a very fine *vaquero*, Teodoro."

"*Gracias.*" Teodoro sounded happy. "But we have to get the horses away from here to our hiding place. I'll go down first. You untie the rope of the pinto and throw it down to me. I'll catch it and snub it around the trunk of another tree and let him fight that. Then throw me the mare's *reata*, and I'll tie her, too."

"They'll attack you, Teodoro."

"I'll keep out of their way. I know how."

Jacinto watched his friend catch the *reatas* and marveled at how easily Teodoro played the plunging horses at the end of the rawhide ropes, edging them cleverly toward the nearest tree. He saw how Teodoro kept out of the reach of striking hooves and long teeth, running around the tree, making the *reatas* fast.

Then Jacinto climbed down. "*Bueno, bueno*," he praised Teodoro. "There should have been six Comanches here to do this thing and you and I have managed."

"There should have been three Mexicans," boasted the other boy.

"What shall we do now?" Jacinto stared up into the night sky. The three-quarters moon was high.

"We let the horses wear themselves out fighting the *reatas*. Then we take them by the ropes and lead them away with us. How did you get so close to the wild horses? I looked for you out on the plain but couldn't see you."

Jacinto showed Teodoro the sling he'd made on the mule. He mounted it and demonstrated how Comanches rode when they wanted to steal up on buffalo herds without being seen or when they were fighting and wanted to protect themselves from enemies. Teodoro got down in the sling but stayed there only a moment.

"It isn't the way *vaqueros* ride," he complained.

"No, but it is useful at times."

Toward morning Teodoro untied the pinto and the

white mare, flinging the ends of each *reata* to Jacinto astride the mule. At first the pinto fought the *reata* until Jacinto brought him alongside the mule. Then he quieted down. The mare was easier to handle than the pinto. The presence of the old mule seemed to calm both wild horses. With Teodoro hanging onto the *reata* of the white horse and Jacinto to that of the other, they set out toward the east.

"I like white horses," said Teodoro, sounding contented.

Jacinto looked back happily at his horse. He'd already noticed that it bore the brand of El Chino Aldama while the mare belonged to Don Quirino. Jacinto was thinking of a name for the pinto—something brave. Soon the horse would know and like him.

"We'll start to break these two tomorrow night," Jacinto told Teodoro.

"A Mexican *vaquero* can break a horse in half a day," Teodoro said with great pride.

"In three days a Comanche can make a willing slave of any wild horse," Jacinto told him.

It took the boys longer than three moonlit nights to gentle the horses. On the second night in the little canyon the Comanche boy roped the pinto by the neck. Then the more skilled Teodoro cast the *reata* around one of the pinto's hind legs. The horse fell to the ground when Teodoro's rope jerked. Both boys flung themselves onto the pinto as the watching mare nickered and reared in fright. While Teodoro held a blindfold over the terrified pinto's eyes, Jacinto put a rawhide halter with a tight nosepiece on him. With *reatas* still on the horse, the boys allowed the pinto to rise and stand trembling in the starlight. Then Teodoro threw the old saddle over his back and cinched it tight.

Next they tied the pinto. Teodoro pulled the horse's head so tight to one side that it was jerked out of normal position. For an hour the pinto was kept tied with his head to the left side, for another hour to the right.

"This is the Mexican way," said Teodoro.

"Now we shall do things as Comanches do," said Jacinto. "I will ride him first."

Mounted on Teodoro's mule, Jacinto led the blindfolded pinto out of the little canyon. Teodoro blocked its entrance with tree branches so the mare couldn't escape, then jumped onto the mule in back of Jacinto. When they reached the Santa Ana, flowing silver in the moonlight, Jacinto ordered his friend to take the pinto out into deep water and gave him the horse's *reata*. When he thought they were deep enough into the river, Jacinto slid down from the mule. He reached for the pinto's saddle horn and swung onto the horse, grabbing the reins. Then Teodoro pulled off the blindfold and let go of the *reata*.

The pinto, once released, went mad with fury. He

never had felt a weight on his back before. Leaping straight up into the air and bucking, he came down splashing and neighing. When he tried to roll in the water to dislodge his rider, Jacinto held his head up by the reins. The pinto plunged backward, standing on his rear legs trying to unseat his rider, but Jacinto hung on. The horse would soon tire in the water.

Teodoro fled on his alarmed mule to the shallows to wait where it was safer. Over the splashings, squealings, and snortings, Jacinto could sometimes hear Teodoro's encouraging shouts.

The pinto had much spirit. It took a long while before he stood quietly in the water. And by then his tender nose was very sore from the rawhide piece clamped over it. Jacinto reached down and jerked on it to the right. The pinto swung his head to the right. The boy jerked to the left, and the horse pulled in that direction. Jacinto moved his legs, touching the pinto with his heels. To his joy the horse started forward toward the bank. When he had climbed out of the river, Jacinto touched him with his heels again, and the pinto sprang forward, running toward the mountains.

He was not a big horse, as California horses were measured, but he was swift. Jacinto delighted in his speed and sure-footedness as the horse raced over the ghostly black-and-white country of tall brooding hills and shadowed plain. The sweetness of sage and the rank smell of wild mustard came to Jacinto's nose as the horse brushed through the plants.

When Jacinto realized that the horse was headed in the direction of the Aldama rancho, he jerked hastily on the nosepiece and turned him around to gallop back to the hiding place. He found Teodoro there waiting in the canyon, sitting on a boulder. The moonlight was bright enough for him to see how anxious his friend's face was.

"I did not fall off," Jacinto said. "The pinto is a fine horse. I will name him Black Hoof." Both boys had noticed that the pinto's right hind hoof was splashed with black.

"I will call my mare Elena," said Teodoro. "It is a pretty name."

"Tomorrow night we'll break her, Teodoro."

"*Sí.*"

Jacinto got down from the sweating pinto. He patted his neck with affection, then stood in front of the horse. There was one more thing he must do to make the pinto truly his. While Teodoro looked on, shocked at Jacinto's foolhardiness, the Comanche boy took the horse's jaw in his hands, lifted it, and breathed into each of the pinto's nostrils.

"Do I have to do *that?*" asked Teodoro. "He could have bitten off your nose."

"No, this is how Comanches tame horses. It is a secret. I have given him my breath. I will break your

mare for you in the river, but because you are not a
Comanche you don't have to breathe into her."

"That's good. I'll tie a load of grass on Black Hoof's
back tomorrow morning. If he carries it around all day,
that will prove he's broken. When Elena carries grass
all day, too, she will be ready for me to ride."

"And then we can go out on the plain together," said
Jacinto, starting to remove Black Hoof's saddle. As soon
as he could, he'd make a Comanche-style halter for him
and ride on a leather pad. He would train the pinto
to let him ride, hanging from the sling. Teodoro could
ride as he chose.

"Spotted Wild Horse," asked Teodoro, "does anyone
from Agua Mansa know that you are leaving the village
at night?"

"No, but the sheep and the goats might." Jacinto
laughed. "Sometimes they come up and nibble at me
when I fall asleep herding them. Does Tío Carlos know
that you leave?"

"I don't think so. Sometimes he's awake when I go
out, but I tell him it's to stop the dog barking or to
look at one of the gamecocks. When I come back, he
is wheezing and his eyes are closed, so I think he must
be asleep."

ON
THE
PLAIN

IX

Breaking the mare was less difficult than breaking
Black Hoof. She was by nature gentler than the pinto.
In a week's time both horses could be ridden anywhere
by the boys, although Black Hoof was sometimes rebel-
lious and ran away with Jacinto.

Once the horses were broken Jacinto and Teodoro
met at the little canyon only during the periods when
the moon was bright. Then they rode across country
together looking for the herds. Some nights they chased
cattle for amusement, with Teodoro grabbing yearlings
by the tail, flinging them head over heels as *vaqueros*
did with full-grown steers. Jacinto took no part in this
game. He practiced riding in his sling so he'd be as
good as any Comanche rider when the time came to

return over the mountains. He didn't mention his dream of escaping Rancho San Bernardino to Teodoro, but always he scouted for the herd with the best horses. He kept practicing with the *reata* while shepherding until he was good enough to rope a running goat by the neck seven out of ten times. And at night he practiced on steers, catching them and releasing them.

While spring wore on and he made adobes for the new church, he thought constantly of Black Hoof and of his plans. He behaved very politely to all of the New Mexicans. Why risk trouble? They were much less polite to him. Many still blamed him for the collapse of the old church. It didn't matter to them that he now went to Mass. Few people were willing to stand or kneel near him on the floor of the seatless, benchless church, except for Santos Gamboa. He or one of his sons sometimes were in Jacinto's row across from Señora Gomez, who stayed on the women's side of the church.

In April visitors came to Agua Mansa during the time of the *matanza* on the plains. They were New Mexican traders who had been in the pueblo of Los Angeles for weeks, dickering for horses, silk cloth, and embroidered shawls from China. On their way back to Santa Fe they stopped to see Santos Gamboa, an old comrade of theirs. He welcomed them though no one in Agua Mansa had anything to sell or trade. When the traders' caravan left, Jacinto noticed that many of the villagers seemed downcast. Carmela Gomez even wept to see them go. They had made her homesick for Taos; one of the men had known her husband well.

"He will take the news to the Gomez family in Taos that my husband is dead," she told Jacinto. "When the trader comes back to California next year, he will bring me news of my family and friends. The trading caravans come each year from New Mexico. This year Don Pedro Aldama himself told them we were here. Last year they passed by Agua Mansa because they did not know that Don Santos lived beside the Santa Ana."

"*Sí, señora.*" Jacinto was thinking his own thoughts. Caravans went each year from New Mexico into Comanche lands, too. Once he returned to New Mexico with his horses, it shouldn't be difficult for him to attach himself to a caravan heading east out of Taos, a place where no one knew him.

"The traders greatly admired our fields and our beautiful river, Jacinto," the woman went on. "And they said our church will be a very fine one. They liked Padre Anton, too, even if he is a foreigner with yellow hair."

"Did they?" Jacinto could hardly believe that traders admired fields.

"*Sí.* Padre Anton asked them about a bell. I heard one of them tell him that they sold copper kettles and iron pots but not church bells. Bells are very heavy and hard to carry. I suppose one could be carried in a wagon, but no wagon can pass over the Spanish Trail, can it? Still, a strong mule might carry a bell if the mule was carefully loaded. The trader said a small church bell can cost as much as sixty Yankee dollars. So, even if a very strong mule could carry it. . . ."

Tired of her chattering, Jacinto yawned and looked toward the window. It was dusk. The Aldama *vaqueros* had completed their *matanza* and roundup only two days before. The plain was strewn with the carcasses of skinned steers. A *vaquero* had ridden through Agua Mansa on the way to the rancho and told a settler that the last of the calves had been branded and the last hide taken. There would be no cowboys on the plain tonight. But there would be a full moon.

Teodoro would know that the *matanza* and roundup were over, too. The boys had agreed not to ride out while it lasted. Teodoro would be watching the moon and would be at the canyon hiding place when Jacinto arrived after Mass.

Although Teodoro owned an old rusty pistol that he was very proud of and Jacinto had his bow, they carried no weapons when they went out on the plain at night. A few nights of riding had taught them that only a man on foot was in any real danger. A rider who never fell off or was thrown was safe, certainly from everything but mountain lions.

Tonight Jacinto on Black Hoof took the lead riding toward the mountains, followed by Teodoro on Elena.

Earlier that evening, just as the setting sun had turned
the sharp hills east of Agua Mansa blood-red, Jacinto
had glanced north. A haze of yellow dust lay beneath
the mountains—horses or cattle running. Jacinto didn't
know which, but more than likely the animals were
horses. Cows chose to wander about in two's or three's.

The boys found that the haze had been made by wild
horses, the particular herd Jacinto secretly liked best.
They were young fleet animals under the rule of a bay
stallion with a white blaze on his face. When he was
ready to escape, Jacinto hoped to take horses from this
herd, particularly some of the fillies that the stallion
had sired and as many pintos as he could capture.

Teodoro had to keep his distance from the wild
horses. Jacinto, riding in the horsehair-rope sling, could
approach the edges of the herd. He wasn't worried
about the horses scenting him. He had rubbed wild
mustard into his clothing, face, and hands before he'd
mounted Black Hoof. Tonight Jacinto practiced spying
on the horses, watching them under Black Hoof's belly.
He knew Teodoro was behind the herd, probably
standing on top of one of the many small hills that
dotted this part of the plain so near the mountains.
If his friend wanted to ride nearer the herd, let him
put a sling on the mare. Teodoro's stubborn insistence
on a saddle cost him the joy of being so near the wild
ones.

The moon tonight reminded Jacinto of a silver real

from which someone had clipped a sliver of metal.
Tomorrow night it would be at its fullest, but tonight
there was plenty of light for Jacinto to admire the
horses and even make out the brand of the Aldamas
and other rancheros on their flanks. Jacinto was urging
Black Hoof closer to a colt that greatly resembled the
bay stallion grazing a short distance away. He glanced
at the stallion and saw the horse jerk up his head. The
leader of the herd stood without moving, his head high,
his nostrils sniffing the night wind. Then he shook his
head and stamped one of his front feet. Jacinto heard
him snorting. The stallion was uneasy.

Had the horse smelled him? No, he didn't come
toward him, ears back, front feet and teeth ready to
attack. Was it Teodoro? Had he come too near and
been seen? The stallion was always on guard. He'd
attack Teodoro. Jacinto was reining Black Hoof away
from the herd's edge when suddenly he heard a new
sound above the stallion's snorts. It was the buzz of a
musket bullet, and it came from behind him—not from
the hills on his right.

Jacinto watched the bay stallion rear and heard him
trumpet to the other horses. They were running as
soon as the stallion had finished signaling them. Wild
horses swept up from behind, surrounding Black Hoof
on all sides. Jacinto became part of the stampede. The
horses were too frightened to take notice of him,
though they ran close enough to brush against him.

Suddenly Jacinto heard yelling over the sounds of the wild horses. Men were shouting, urging the herd onward to the northeast. Rising up by his heel, Jacinto risked a look over Black Hoof's back. At first all he could see were the rumps, shoulders, and backs of the wild horses. Then beyond them he spied riders. They rode with ropes twirling, screeching at a high note that maddened the herd.

Utes! They'd come again. They'd ridden in from the west, stealing up on the herd. And suddenly Jacinto knew in his heart what the musket shot meant. It had not been fired to get the wild horses running. It had been aimed at Teodoro, who was riding a white horse and wearing a large Mexican hat, always being as much like a *vaquero* as he could.

Jacinto didn't know how far Black Hoof ran with the herd until the Utes stopped yelling and the wild horses slowed. He tried to ease the pinto out of the herd to the south, but a Ute riding there drove Black Hoof back, not seeing Jacinto. The boy was tiring in his awkward riding position. His arm ached, and he knew if he rode much farther he wouldn't be able to pull himself up by his heel. There was only one thing for him to do—drop back in the herd as far as possible and fall off, hoping the Utes wouldn't see him. He would lose Black Hoof, but he might save his life.

Praying to the god of the Comanches, Jacinto pulled back on Black Hoof's reins. Obediently the pinto, which trotted among the wild horses as weary as they were, slowed and dropped farther and farther back. When Jacinto saw there were only a few horses behind him, he pulled his arm out of the rope sling, let go with his heel, and thumped to the ground. Horses wouldn't step on a man lying on the ground if they could avoid it. Now if only the last Utes would pass him by. Jacinto lay flat on the ground, face down, his heart racing, hoping his sheepskin jacket wouldn't be seen.

His hope was blasted by a cry. "*Quat'z! Quat'z!*" Before he could get to his feet to run, three raiders stood over him on horseback, three muskets pointed down at him. Jacinto lay there until another man came riding up. He saw the necklace of grizzly teeth on his chest. He was the same man he'd seen watering his horse in the Santa Ana. The man who might be Walkara, the Ute chief.

"Get up," ordered the chief in Spanish.

"*Quat'z?*" asked another Ute.

The chief leaned forward to look Jacinto over very carefully. He asked in Spanish, "Are you *Quat'z*, an iron shirt, a Mexican?" He came so close that Jacinto could have touched his horse. "No, you have the look of a *Komant'z*." His hand went to the bowie knife at his belt.

Jacinto stared at him. He knew a Ute would rather have a Comanche scalp than any other. And how he

would like to take a Ute scalp home with him! But he
was glad that he didn't have his bow with him. One
glance at it and at his arrows would tell any Ute that
a Comanche had made them.

"What are you?" demanded the chief.

"*Quat'z*, a Mexican," Jacinto replied in Spanish.

One of the raiders, with the letter *C* branded on his
chin, spoke in the Ute language and pointed behind
him. The chief nodded, then asked Jacinto, "The boy
who was riding the white horse was *Quat'z* also?"

Jacinto's heart stopped for a sickening instant. Teodoro! The musket shot had killed him. The raiders
must have thought he was someone guarding the herd
for the rancheros. Anger rose up over Jacinto's fright.
He wanted to drag the Ute chief from his horse and
kill him, too. But he knew that before he could do so
one of the Utes would shoot him.

Jacinto didn't move. He scarcely breathed while the
Utes spoke together. Then the chief asked, "Why are
you here? You are only a boy."

"I was riding a horse."

"You came to steal a horse?"

Why not tell the Ute chief the truth? "*Sí*."

The man laughed. "Utes take horses—all horses here.
They do not want boys of the *Quat'z* people. You are
too big to sell as a slave, and you are too small to fight."

"I am not too small to fight," Jacinto flared.

"For a Ute you are too small. There is no spirit in

Mexicans. Iron shirt you are, no shirt you will be." The chief laughed. He gave an order to the raider nearest him, the man with the brand on his chin. He jumped down from his horse, came up to Jacinto, jerked the boy's knife from him, and put it into his own sash. Then he pointed to Jacinto's jacket. Jacinto took it off. The raider jabbed his thumb at his shirt, and Jacinto took it off too, then his trousers and finally his boots. The man grabbed up the discarded clothing and stuffed it into his saddlebags, all the while laughing and joking with the other raiders.

Finally the three men, led by their chief, trotted off toward the disappearing herd, leaving Jacinto standing naked in the moonlight. Through his fury and humiliation, he realized that this treatment was how the Utes showed their contempt for all Mexicans. No, they wouldn't shoot him as they'd shot Teodoro, his friend. But by leaving him defenseless and afoot on the plain, they'd condemned him to death.

Whatever he did, Jacinto knew he couldn't stay where he was. He didn't try to go back to find Teodoro. The herd had galloped far. He headed at a run for the nearest hill. At least there he wouldn't be seen by wild bulls. But he didn't run for long. After only a hundred yards vicious buckthorns studded his feet. He had to pick his way to the hill through brush where spines or prickles of plants wounded him.

The fall of the moon found him near the top of the hill with his feet and legs bleeding from sharp rocks and cruel plants. Climbing the hill had been terrible work, because the rocks kept falling back beneath him, making him slide. By dawn he was at the top, shivering in the cold beneath a pile of rocks pointing to the sky. The colors of the dawn over the plain were pale blue and gold. When Jacinto looked toward the mountains, he could see nothing of the Utes or the wild horses. By now they were going through Cajon Pass on their way to their own country. They had not sent a rider back looking for him, which meant they hadn't spied the horsehair sling on Black Hoof. Utes would recognize it in an instant as the work of a Comanche.

At last Jacinto collapsed, resting his head on his arms. Tears came to his eyes. Everything was lost. Teodoro, his only friend, dead, and Black Hoof stolen. He had never thought he would capture and break a horse only to have it stolen by the Utes. And he, a Comanche, had seen Utes twice and had yet to strike one blow against them. He'd even denied being a Comanche. For a time Jacinto wept, leaning his back against the side of one of the perpendicular rocks. Then he looked out over the countryside again. He'd try to reach the Santa Ana later in the day.

No, there was nothing to be seen on the plain except the reddish decaying corpses of slaughtered steers and

some brown cattle grazing not far from the site of the
matanza. Cattle would be no help. A person couldn't
ride one without a halter. Jacinto stared mournfully
at the animals, wishing that one of them was Black
Hoof. Then suddenly he wiped the mist from his eyes.
Cattle, no! The animals below were brown, but they
weren't cattle. They were large bears—two of them—
down from the mountains, attracted by the smell of
the flayed steers.

Jacinto got to his feet. The movement sent a shower
of little rocks down the side of the hill. The nearest
bear stopped, rose up on its hind legs, and stared in
Jacinto's direction. It was a grizzly. The boy knew it
couldn't see him, but it could scent him. To his horror
he watched the grizzly drop to all fours and start toward
the hill, its nose to the ground, snuffling. He saw it
cross his trail and pause at a flat rock where Jacinto had
stopped to look at his bleeding feet. The grizzly sniffed
the rock for a time, then with more speed passed beyond it and started up the hillside.

Jacinto didn't even try to be quiet. He looked up at
the rocks above him, estimating their height. Running
around them, he found a place he could get one foot
into, then pulled himself up into it and frantically
began to climb. Cut and bruised by the sharpness of
the granite, Jacinto finally got himself up onto the top-
most rock. He clung to it, dangling his feet over the

edge, praying that he would be above the grizzly's reach.

Both bears were now at the top of the hill. They reared up and gazed at Jacinto out of their small scarlet eyes. The larger, a female, raked at the rocks with her horrible claws while her nearly grown cub tried to climb the nearest rock. It was too steep for bear paws, and the female could not reach Jacinto, only growl and paw at him, missing his feet by a short distance.

The sun rose higher. The bears did not leave, though Jacinto knew they must have had their fill of rotting steer flesh. He didn't think they would go away. They were interested in him, this odd "animal" that had run from them and climbed rocks but still stayed in their field of vision. He tried not to look down at the bears but over the plain, praying to the god of the Comanches for help. By now Señora Gomez would be looking everywhere for him and have the entire village hunting, too. Tío Carlos would have missed Teodoro. But Jacinto's hope, he knew, lay with the Widow Gomez. Tío Carlos might not be too disturbed by his grandson's absence. Señora Gomez, though, would go to Santos Gamboa. Gamboa would want to know why he had not taken the goats and sheep out to graze.

Jacinto kept watching the plain until midday. By now he was very thirsty and, far worse, dizzy at times. He couldn't believe his eyesight at first when he saw

the dust cloud in the southern distance. For once he
hoped that it wasn't caused by another herd of wild
horses. If instead it was made by cows with calves
among them, the calves might lure the bears away to
new and better sport.

But no, what emerged from the dust wasn't horses or
cattle, but riders. And not Utes again. These men wore
broad-brimmed hats. Mexicans. *Vaqueros.* Jacinto
pulled himself up on top of his rock. Waving his arms,
he shouted, wishing he had a pistol to fire.

The riders, six of them, halted below his hill. Then
one detached himself from the others, rode up the hill
a way, and took off his hat, waving it. His long hair
shone snow-white in the sunlight, and sunlight glittered
on the mountings of the long rifle he held across his
saddle. Joshua Dove, the Yankee!

Jacinto pointed to the hill below him. He cupped
his hand to his mouth and cried, *"Osos! Osos!* (Bears)!"

Once more Dove waved his hat. Jacinto watched the
old man dismount and come slowly up the hill, his
Kentucky rifle under his arm. The other riders, men
Jacinto didn't know by sight because their hats shadowed their faces, kept at a distance. Jacinto understood
why they stayed behind. Don Joshua was hunting
cabibs.

From his perch Jacinto watched the grizzlies. The
female had taken her attention from him when she
heard the sound of rocks falling on the hill. Something

was moving below her. Jacinto saw her hurry silently to the shelter of some big rocks not far away. She meant to leap out on Dove when he came up to them. By now the American was close enough to hear Jacinto shout, "*Oso*, Don Joshua! *Oso* between the rocks!"

When the grizzly came hurtling out toward Dove, her forepaws raised to maul and crush him, the hunter was ready for her. He stood his ground, raised his rifle, and fired. Jacinto watched the grizzly, shot through the mouth, fall onto the hillside and start to roll down. The shot sent the other bear running down the side of the hill.

Then one of the *vaqueros* darted out from among the others, a *reata* whirling over his head. Jacinto didn't recognize the cowboy, but he knew the brown horse he rode. It was Don Quirino's famous Huechino. The *vaquero* came upon the galloping bear in the open. His *reata* caught the grizzly around the neck but didn't stop him. The bear rose up bellowing, clawing at the rawhide. Then Jacinto saw why the brown horse was so valued. The ordinary-appearing animal was indeed like a cat. His rider didn't have to play the bear himself. He ran in toward the grizzly, taunting him, then darted out, drawing the *reata* tight around the bear's neck while the Mexicans cried their approval. Jacinto forgot about Joshua Dove as he watched the cowboy and Huechino fight the grizzly, keeping always just out of reach of the dreadful claws. Finally the *vaquero* drew his pistol from his sash, rode in within the grizzly's reach, and just as the bear was about to claw him out of the saddle shot him in the head.

After the cheering and cries of "Huechino, Huechino" had stopped, Jacinto heard Joshua Dove calling up to him. "What're you doin' up there with no clothes on?"

"The Utes came last night. I think it was Walkara. They took horses. Utes killed Teodoro and took everything I had."

"Come on down here, Jacinto."

Jacinto came down, skinning his elbows and knees, to where the old man waited for him. By now the *vaqueros* had ridden up to the hilltop. El Chino was with them. He looked at Jacinto and laughed. "We killed steers here to entice bears down from the mountains, but we did not expect to find you here—a boy with no clothing, sitting on rocks to enjoy the view. What are you doing so far from Agua Mansa? Were you bait for the grizzlies, too?"

Jacinto bit his lip. El Chino understood nothing. "The Utes took my clothes last night, and they ran off a herd of your horses."

"Utes! They came again?" El Chino's voice was high with excitement. "What time last night did they come?"

"About midnight," Jacinto told him. "They took many horses up into the mountains."

El Chino spoke to the *vaqueros*. "We'll follow them."

"*No!*" Jacinto ran forward and caught the young man's reins. "There are many Utes. They have muskets and pistols. A chief leads them."

"Walkara himself!" cried El Chino. He put spurs to his horse, swinging it about the narrow space on the hilltop. Its shoulder knocked Jacinto onto the ground as young Aldama started down the hillside followed by the yelling *vaqueros*.

"Stop him, Don Joshua!" cried Jacinto to the old Yankee, who had jumped back as El Chino's horse had turned.

"I'd jest as soon try to stop the devil wind as that El Chino." He prodded Jacinto with his hand. "Come on, boy, we got to go tell Gamboa and Don Quirino about the raiders. We can ride double. There's a canteen o' water tied to my saddle. You got to be thirsty."

As Jacinto hobbled down the slope on his wounded feet, the next words of the old bear hunter blistered themselves into his mind. They even drove away the thoughts of pain in his feet and his grief over the loss of Teodoro and Black Hoof. "Jacinto, you don' have to try to tell me that you and Teodoro wasn' out ridin' hosses you stole from the Aldamas. They're gonna know it, too. You bet. There ain't no other way you two woulda been this far out here toward the mountains. You think you been in trouble. It ain't nothin' to the trouble you're gonna be in purty soon. I woulda thought you'd be smarter."

THE
JUDGE
OF
THE
PLAIN

X

At Dove's house the old man stopped only long enough to snatch one of his shirts from his wife's clothesline and hand it to Jacinto. The boy squirmed into it riding double behind Dove.

"Who'll go to find Teodoro?" Jacinto asked the Yankee a moment later.

"Somebody from the rancho with a cart. Tell me where you left him."

Jacinto gave Dove the landmarks where he and Teodoro had joined the herd and Teodoro had stayed behind.

As they rode into Agua Mansa Dove shouted for Santos Gamboa. At once his horse was surrounded by New Mexicans, staring at Jacinto's odd costume and eager to hear what Don Joshua wanted. Gamboa hurried from the site of the new church with Padre Anton coming after him.

Watching Gamboa approach made Jacinto want to vanish into the air. What would Gamboa do to him? But when Jacinto got down from Dove's horse, he was caught and held not by Santos Gamboa but by his son, Hipolito. The Widow Gomez came pushing through the crowd toward them.

She cried, "Where have you been, Jacinto? Who's shirt is that?"

Jacinto didn't answer her. Dove spoke for him but not until all the settlers had gathered within hearing. "Jacinto, here, went out hoss ridin' with the Ramirez boy last night. The Utes come and run off the herd o' wild hosses they was ridin' near. Seems they shot Teodoro and turned Jacinto loose after they stole his clothes. We spotted him on a hill bein' scouted for fresh meat by two cabibs. A *vaquero* and me, we got rid o' them bears. The *vaqueros* lit out after the Utes, so I come here to tell ya, Don Santos."

Gamboa's eyes were flat as he gave Jacinto one look that made the boy step back in spite of himself. In Comanche he asked, "You stole horses of the Aldamas?"

"Yes, I did what a Comanche would do."

"The Aldamas may kill you. They have the right."

"*Sí*, I know."

Gamboa turned away and gave orders to the settlers,

who would pursue the raiders again. Then he said to Dove, "Don Joshua, will you ride to the rancho and give the alarm?"

"I surely will." Dove shook his head. "That young fool El Chino headed for the mountains with only four *vaqueros*. Jacinto says there was plenty o' Utes."

"That is like El Chino—to be a fool," Gamboa spoke flatly. "It may cost him his life." Now the leader of the New Mexicans turned to the priest. "Padre, will you take Jacinto to see Tío Carlos? I think he should tell the old man how his grandson died. Take the white mare. Jacinto is very fond of horses. Mules are not good enough for him."

"I'll take him as soon as he's properly dressed." Padre Anton put his hand on Jacinto's shoulder and propelled him forward out of the crowd. The settlers made way for the priest, but as Jacinto passed by them he heard the angry murmurs directed at him.

A woman said to another, "He laughs when the church falls down, and he steals horses from Don Quirino. *Ay de mí*, let the Aldamas rid us of him. He has a devil in him."

Jacinto said nothing to the priest or to Señora Gomez, who was crying as she brought out his best shirt and trousers and his moccasins. He wouldn't let her embrace him. He wouldn't accept even a *tortilla* from her, though he was very hungry.

When he'd climbed up onto the old mare behind the

priest and they were on the way to the Ramirez house, he finally broke his silence. "After I have told Tío Carlos, will you take me to the Aldama rancho?"

"Is that what you want?"

"*Sí*. If I do not go myself, Don Quirino will send men after me. He will know that Teodoro and I stole his horses."

"Perhaps Joshua Dove will not tell him?"

"Even if he doesn't, Don Quirino will guess. Everyone has."

"This El Chino and the *vaqueros* didn't accuse you, did they?"

Jacinto shook his head. Each time El Chino was mentioned, his sorrow deepened. "El Chino will die, too," he told Padre Anton.

The priest sighed as the old mare stumbled. Jacinto had noticed that Padre Anton was a poor rider. Although yesterday he would have felt contempt, he didn't care now. "I will pray that the *vaqueros* and Don Quirino's son will return safely." The priest was silent for a time, then asked, "You were in very great danger from the Utes and bears. Did you pray?"

"*Sí*, to the god of my people."

"Not to San Salvador?"

"No, padre, I did not think of him."

They rode in silence to the Ramirez house where both dismounted. The priest led the mare to the door.

Tío Carlos came out at Padre Anton's call. Standing

in the doorway, he gazed at Jacinto, then the priest. He rested one hand on the side of the door and said, "Teodoro did not come home with you?"

Padre Anton would have said something comforting, but Jacinto spoke first. "The Utes killed Teodoro last night while we were riding. I think Walkara was the one who led them. There was an Indian with him who had a letter of the alphabet branded on his face. It was a *C*."

"Walkara, and a man with a brand on his face? You and Teodoro were riding?"

"Teodoro and I stole horses." Jacinto corrected himself. "*I* stole a horse. Teodoro only borrowed one. He meant to return her to the herd. I was going to run away over the mountains on mine."

"How did you get these horses?"

"From a herd. We captured and broke them."

"You and Teodoro? Only the two of you?"

"*Sí.*"

"And now he is dead—and you are alive. The Utes didn't kill you? Why?"

Jacinto nodded in his misery. "I don't know why. They made some sort of joke with me. They left me so Don Quirino could kill me."

"He has the right to do that."

"*Sí.*" Jacinto looked at the cages of gamecocks and at the Ramirez dog lying in the warm sunshine by the side of the house. The day was so very bright. Teodoro couldn't be dead. "I am sorry," said Jacinto, using these words for the first time in his life.

Tío Carlos was staring over the boy's head at a hawk circling in the sky. "It is the country here. It is hard, too hard. Only the herds truly thrive here. After my wife sickened and died, my son and his wife were killed by Indians from the desert. Now the Utes have taken my grandson. It is the land. I knew the man with the brand on his face. He was a Mission Indian from the *asistencia* who ran away and became an outlaw. The letter *C* is for *cimarrón* (fugitive). He was branded by order of Don Pedro Aldama years ago."

Padre Anton put out his hand to comfort the old man. "Come to Agua Mansa. A wake for Teodoro will be held there. He will be buried on the bluff above the new church. Joshua Dove has gone to the Aldamas to warn them of the Utes and to send *vaqueros* after your grandson's body."

"In time I will come, padre. *Gracias*." Tío Carlos wasn't weeping. Jacinto saw with much wonder how calm he was. "What will you do?" he suddenly asked Jacinto.

"Go to the rancho before Don Quirino sends men to get me."

"That is wise," said the old Mexican. "Go with God. If Don Quirino frees you, come visit me wherever I am. I'd like to hear how you and Teodoro captured and broke wild horses. That is not work for boys."

Jacinto swung about and buried his face against the neck of the mare. He'd rather go to the rancho than sit beside Teodoro's coffin, knowing the people of Agua Mansa hated him. At the wake they'd whisper within his hearing that he'd "murdered" his friend.

"*Sí*, it is the land," he heard Tío Carlos telling Padre Anton once more. "It is too rich. Too many men want its riches. First the Indians owned it. The Spaniards took it from them, and the Mexicans from the Spaniards. I think someday the Yankees will take it from the Mexicans."

"Yes," said the priest, "I believe you are right."

Don Quirino Aldama didn't speak at all with Jacinto personally. Joshua Dove had ridden away, and Aldama was too busy ordering more *vaqueros* to follow his son, telling them to take the best horses from his corral. He talked briefly with Padre Anton, though, in the dim high-ceilinged room that served him as a reception room and office.

After one sharp flicking glance at Jacinto, Don Quirino said to the priest, "Don Joshua Dove tells me this Indian boy stole one of my horses, padre." Aldama's voice was harsh.

"He is only a boy, Don Quirino."

"He is not an infant. He will be punished." The man spoke to the Indian manservant waiting in a corner of the room. "Confine this thief somewhere until I can judge him. I have more important things on my mind now."

"Do not lose courage," whispered the priest, as Jacinto was led off by the Indian servant.

Jacinto was locked up in a small outbuilding where old saddles were kept on pegs. It was dark and hot by day and cold by night. No one came near him but the same Indian servant with food and water. On the second night while he sat on the floor, shivering, wishing for a blanket, the Indian spoke to him for the first time. "Huechino has come back."

"What of the *vaqueros?*"

"Only the horse returned. The *patrón* thinks the *vaqueros* who went with his son must be dead."

Jacinto tensed himself. "Why does he say that?"

"Because Huechino had an arrow in him. The *vaqueros* must have found the Utes. The *patrón* has sent a rider to the pueblo in Los Angeles asking old Don Pedro to come here at once."

"Why should he come?"

"Because he is head of the Aldama family. So, it will be Don Pedro who judges you, not Don Quirino. Don Pedro will be Judge of the Plain when he comes." The servant went out, locking the door behind him.

Don Pedro! Jacinto thought of the stern old Mexican he'd seen at El Cobarde's first cockfight. He was not at all like Tío Carlos. He ordered that boys who didn't take off their hats to him be whipped. How would he deal with a horse thief? At the end of a rope, Jacinto suspected.

Sí, let Don Pedro sentence him to death if he wished.

Jacinto thought much as he sat alone in the dark. He'd talked Teodoro into stealing horses. He was as much to blame for his friend's death as the Ute who'd killed him. In his mind Jacinto went over the months he'd lived on Rancho San Bernardino. He never had become a part of the life of Agua Mansa. Santos Gamboa had been fair to him, fairer than he'd been to Gamboa. Probably the man always had known what he planned to do. One Comanche would understand another. And Jacinto had misjudged Mexicans. Not all were tricksters who thought they were magicians. Teodoro hadn't been. Señora Gomez, who was half-Mexican, was just and kind. As for Tío Carlos, he'd even asked him to come back to see him and talk of Teodoro and horses. Tío Carlos had not said one word of blame to him for his grandson's death.

Now Jacinto had no more desire to take horses and return to New Mexico. His surly behavior in the house of Delacruz had cost him greatly. If he'd behaved better there, Delacruz would not have sent him away. New Mexico was far closer to Comanche country. From there he could have escaped easily. He was too far away here to make the attempt. A man alone could not travel the many dangerous miles of the Spanish Trail. Even if Don Pedro spared his life, he wouldn't try to run off.

He would not have a horse again. He would try to become a farmer like the other New Mexicans, if they'd have him in their village again.

The boy escaped from his unhappy thoughts only in his sleep. In dreams sometimes he heard the bells of Santa Fe. They gave him some peace from nightmares of Utes and stampeding horses.

On the third evening the servant came at last to get Jacinto. He brought him into the house to the same room where the boy had seen Don Quirino. Sitting behind a table with Don Quirino beside him was Don Pedro. There were three other chairs in the room. On one perched Padre Anton, looking uncomfortable. On another, bent and small, sat Tío Carlos. And on the third was Joshua Dove, dressed in a long black coat and trousers with his hat on his knees. Santos Gamboa stood, his arms folded, behind the Yankee. Jacinto stared from face to face. Candlelight was warm and golden, but it did little to soften the men's faces. All looked very serious. Jacinto's legs began to tremble more.

Suddenly Aldama's American agent opened a door and came in. "Do you want him to pay his respects first, Don Pedro?" he asked.

"Yes, show him."

Ross crooked a finger at Jacinto, who followed him out of the room. The Yankee led him to a very large shadowy room filled with black-clad women sitting in rows on stools. A coffin lay on a trestle in the center of the room. Wax candles in very tall brass candlesticks surrounded the coffin. Jacinto went forward slowly when Ross pushed him. He looked down into the coffin at El Chino, who lay with his hands folded on his breast. The young man's face was pinched and white and his head bound around with a black silk cloth. Like his father and grandfather, he was dressed in black.

"The Utes killed him and the *vaqueros* with him," said Ross. "I have heard from old Dove that you cried out to Serafin not to follow the raiders. He says Serafin would not listen to you."

Jacinto nodded. He asked very softly, "Did Gamboa and the other *vaqueros* catch the Utes?"

"No, they got away. They had too much of a start this time. Except for Huechino, the horses Serafin and his men rode were taken, too, after the men were shot. All of the men were scalped."

Sí, that explained the black bandage, thought Jacinto.

Ross went on, "The four cowboys were buried in Cajon Pass. El Chino was brought home. *Vaqueros* climbed high into the mountains for snow after they had killed a stray steer and skinned him. They filled the hide with snow, put El Chino into it, and rode here with him. Come now. Don Pedro is waiting for you."

They left the wake and went back to the room. Old Aldama asked Jacinto at once, "You are named Jacinto Delacruz of Agua Mansa, a shepherd?"

"*Sí, patrón.*"

"You were once a houseservant to Don Hilario Delacruz of Santa Fe and before that a Comanche Indian captive named Spotted Wild Horse?"

"*Sí, patrón.* I am still a Comanche."

"So Santos Gamboa tells me," said Don Pedro. He gestured toward the men. "All speak for you—the priest because he is a priest and all priests seek, of course, to do good. It is to be expected of them. Tío Carlos says 'boys certainly will ride horses that do not belong to them.'" Don Pedro snorted. "Santos Gamboa tells me that it is 'deep in the nature of all young Comanche boys to take horses.' Did you plan to return this horse? Did the Ramirez boy plan to return his?"

"Teodoro did, *patrón.* I meant to escape someday and go back to my people."

Don Pedro coughed. "You are honest, even if you are a horse thief." He leaned forward, his dark eyes intent on Jacinto's face. "Don Joshua says that you tried to stop my grandson from chasing the Utes."

"*Sí,* I told him there were too many raiders."

Don Quirino broke in. "Why did the Utes permit you to live when they killed the Ramirez boy and my son and the *vaqueros*?"

"The chief joked with the others. He said I was too

small to fight and too big to sell as a slave. The Utes called me a *Quat'z*, an iron shirt. That's their name for a Mexican, isn't it?"

Don Pedro nodded while Jacinto watched the huge shadow the man cast on the whitewashed wall behind him. "The Spanish soldiers and explorers that the Utes first saw wore metal breastplates and helmets. They knew they came from Mexico. That was nearly three hundred years ago, but no matter. They still use the name for us."

Jacinto went on. "Then the chief told an Indian to take my shirt and everything else I had. They didn't want my scalp, *patrón*."

"They meant to kill the boy," Joshua Dove interrupted, "leaving him naked like he was born and without no knife. Don' tell me them Utes didn' know there was grizzlies comin' down out o' the hills after your *matanza* meat."

"Very likely the Utes meant for the boy to die. That would be the sort of thing Walkara would enjoy," said Ross.

"The chief of the Utes didn't know Jacinto is a Comanche," added Gamboa. "If he had, the boy's age would have made no difference."

Jacinto sighed. "Señor Gamboa, they asked me if I was a Comanche. I said I was a Mexican."

"So! That was very noble of you!" exclaimed Don

Pedro. "I hope it didn't offend you too much to make such a claim."

Jacinto mumbled, "There are no Comanches here in California, only Genizaros."

"Ah." The head of the Aldama family slammed his hand down on the table. "And I am told you are not a Genizaro at all! Not a Christian! Do you know that I can order a *vaquero* to tie a *reata* around your waist and drag you to your death behind a galloping horse?"

"*Sí, patrón,* I know."

The old Judge of the Plain shook his head. "But I shall not give such an order, though if you dare to steal another horse I promise you this will be done to you. As I have told you, boy, all of the men here have spoken in your behalf, telling me how young you are and asking mercy for you. The priest tells me that he calls you by your Comanche name. It is shameful that you have him do so. He tells me, too, that you live with an old woman in the village of the New Mexicans. She did not watch over you well. You no longer will live with her and be spoiled by her. And you *will* be called Jacinto Delacruz. You claimed to be a Mexican before the Utes. So be it. Do not try to escape your name anymore. As you said, there are no Comanches here. You will live with the priest. Until his house is ready for him, you will live with Santos Gamboa. You will serve Padre Anton as his servant and I hope in time become a Christian. Perhaps he can tame you. No one else seems to have been able to."

"But who will herd the sheep and goats?" Jacinto asked, too surprised by Don Pedro's remarks to say *gracias*.

"Someone else," said Gamboa. "You will serve the priest as Don Pedro orders. Tío Carlos is coming to live in Agua Mansa in the house of the Widow Gomez."

Jacinto thought for a long moment. He asked politely, "Don Santos, am I still to help with the building of the church?"

"That you must ask Padre Anton," said Gamboa.

The priest got up. The other men rose, too. Jacinto bowed to Padre Anton, watching Don Pedro out of the corner of one eye. "I will serve you, padre. I will make adobes, too."

"So be it," remarked the priest calmly. He bowed to the Aldamas, then followed Ross out of the room, his fingers on the rosary at his belt.

Jacinto watched Don Joshua shake hands with the two Aldamas. Gamboa bowed low to them. Jacinto copied him, bowing first to Don Pedro, then to Don Quirino. He remembered to say, *"Muchas gracias, patrónes."*

Gamboa, Dove, and Jacinto left the house together and went to the corral where Dove's horse, the old white mare, and a mule Jacinto recognized as coming from Agua Mansa waited. The New Mexican gestured toward it. "The mule is for you to ride."

Jacinto was surprised. "You were so certain Don Pedro would let me go that you brought a mule for me?"

"Not so sure by a long shot," answered Dove. "If ya got yerself dragged to death, we'd planned to bury ya on the bluff next to Teodoro. Mules'll carry bodies more willing than horses. Anyhow this here animal needed to trot some of the lard outa him. Ya know, Jacinto, you got off real easy back there. You seen Mexican justice now. What d'ya think of it? It's fast, but I always found it fair and square."

"It is fair, Don Joshua." Jacinto mounted the mule. He rode close behind the two men, deep in thought. *Sí*, he owed his life to them and to Padre Anton. If they hadn't spoken for him, Don Pedro would have had him dragged to death. Jacinto was grateful. After thinking about his strange trial, he decided he'd try to serve Padre Anton as well as he could.

Halfway to Agua Mansa under a waning moon, he asked, "Why didn't Padre Anton come with us?"

Dove answered, "He hasta stay behind to say the right buryin' words over El Chino. He'll be buried in the graveyard outside the ranch house. I don' know what kinda words they'd be."

"A funeral Mass," said Santos Gamboa.

"Them's the right words. My wife'd know. She's Catholic. She sure takes to Padre Anton."

Jacinto listened to the men talking while he thought about the cemetery beside the ranch house. Teodoro had told him on one of their moonlight rides that his mother and father lay there, victims of raiders. As Tío Carlos had said, California was a hard land. But there was justice in it. Don Pedro Aldama had shown him more justice than he really deserved.

In the days that followed Jacinto found life in Agua Mansa different. Señora Gomez was still friendly, but she kept her distance. He knew Gamboa had spoken to her about him. She was occupied with old Tío Carlos, who was more feeble than ever and required much care and proper food. Santos Gamboa had moved the old Mexican and his dog into the Gomez house personally. The gamecocks had been given to Don Quirino along with the old mule. Tío Carlos complained that the Widow Gomez fussed over him day and night, nagging him. But all the same he seemed to grow in strength.

Another boy shepherded the flocks while Jacinto trailed Padre Anton from place to place, running errands for him. He helped him into his vestments to say Mass. He helped lay adobes for the church and the priest's house, and finally the padre and the boy worked side by side on the roof of the church, interweaving tules and pouring tar. Each day at sunset, though, Jacinto left Padre Anton to climb the bluff to the graveyard. There he stood for a time, looking down at the wooden cross marked *Teodoro Ramirez* in black paint. He knew what the words below the name said: *Rogad por su alma.* (Pray for his soul.) Jacinto didn't pray, though he mourned his friend. No, he was not a Genizaro. Each time Jacinto left he placed a little pebble beside the cross to mark his visit. Others from the village came, too. Over the weeks the pile of pebbles left by mourners grew higher.

One summer night even Padre Anton seemed mournful. He sat in the small house the settlers had built for him next to the church, darning a hole in his vestments. Jacinto and he had moved in the week before.

"Jacinto," the priest said abruptly.

"*Sí*, padre, do you want something?" Jacinto started to get up from the corner where he sat braiding rawhide to make a mule halter.

"No, I don't want anything. Did you hear the wind this morning?"

"*Sí*." The wind had blown early in the day, a cool one from the west and very welcome after days of dry heat.

"It made me think all day of my home in Switzerland. Last night I dreamed again of my home because I heard the bells in my sleep."

"Do they have bells in Switzerland, padre?"

The priest laughed. "Ah, Jacinto, do they have bells! Great bells with beautiful voices, each one different. There are many churches in my country. In the mountain air, how the bells sound! They can be heard for many leagues."

"They have bells in Santa Fe, too. I liked them."

"Tell me about them."

Jacinto spoke wistfully of the bells he remembered, knowing that he would never hear them again. But neither would Padre Anton hear the bells in Switzerland. He'd shown Jacinto a map of the world in a book he had. Switzerland was unbelievably far away from California, much farther than Santa Fe or Comanche lands. Only a ship, something Jacinto had never seen and could scarcely comprehend, could take the priest home again.

"I would like to have a bell for our church," said Padre Anton.

Jacinto smiled. "But there is no bell tower."

"That is true. But bells don't have to be hung in bell towers. A bell can hang on a timber placed between two trees. We have two trees near the church that are the right distance apart."

Amazed at such a thought, Jacinto argued, "The Widow Gomez said a church bell cost sixty Yankee dollars. The New Mexico traders told her. They would certainly know."

Padre Anton bit off the thread. "Perhaps we could find sixty dollars for a bell?"

"How, padre?"

"By going about begging." He grinned at the alarmed expression on Jacinto's face. "We priests are not above begging for what we need, though I imagine you Comanches are."

"We steal what we want." Jacinto flushed after he'd blurted this admission.

Only Padre Anton, Tío Carlos, the Widow Gomez, and the Gamboa family never mentioned his stealing a horse to Jacinto's face. Other people in Agua Mansa weren't so kind. They called him "horse thief." Many thought he would bring bad luck. Some of the children turned their backs as he passed and crossed themselves when Padre Anton wasn't walking with him. Jacinto knew their parents had told them to protect themselves in this manner from his evil gaze.

"I will go begging with you," the boy told Padre Anton, though he knew he would hate doing so. Having a bell would please Don Santos and Tío Carlos. Señora Gomez would be beyond herself with delight. Certainly the thought of Jacinto's begging would amuse Joshua Dove. The old Yankee thought Padre Anton was very entertaining anyway. What would Dove have to say to the crazy idea of a bell hanging between two trees?

"A bell will be a very fine signal in case the raiders

come again. Even from his house Don Joshua could hear it ringing," said Padre Anton, rethreading his needle.

"The Aldamas are too far away to hear it," Jacinto commented.

"No matter. Don Quirino will give me some money for our bell. We will go there first of all."

Jacinto let the length of rawhide fall onto his lap. Sixty dollars was a great deal of money. The Aldamas, like other rancheros, had hides and sometimes tallow to trade with Yankees, who loaded such things on their ships. But they didn't have gold or silver. They spent the money the Yankees gave them in the pueblo of Los Angeles for cloth and other supplies they could not raise on the rancho. Californians had few coins. They didn't really need them. Everyone knew this—everyone but this priest from Switzerland. He was crazy.

THE
BELL

XI

Padre Anton and Jacinto went by mule first to the
Aldama rancho, where the boy waited inside the corral
because he didn't want to see Don Quirino again.
After one glance at the cemetery near the house, he
looked away. That glance had shown him the new
cross, marking El Chino's grave. It reminded him of
Teodoro and of El Cobarde and even of Black Hoof.
His longing for the horse had been joined by a new
surge of sadness for the gamecock Teodoro had given
him.

Don Quirino donated some money for the bell—
Yankee silver dollars, some reales, and other coins
Jacinto couldn't even identify. The sum came to less

than eight dollars in Yankee money, but Aldama
claimed it was all he had on hand.

"If we fare so badly here, how will we do among the
poor people?" the priest asked Jacinto.

"Much worse, padre."

At Joshua Dove's house they got less money. In
Agua Mansa they had no luck at all, except for some
reales the settlers had brought from New Mexico.

"It seems to be hopeless," Jacinto heard Padre Anton
tell Santos Gamboa. "I have gathered only the amount
of twelve dollars."

"*Sí*, we have crops, and the Aldamas have horses
and cattle, but we have no gold or silver. What we
had, you now have. Farmers see few coins." Gamboa
nodded after he'd spoken.

The priest said heavily, "Then, Santos, I must return
the money. Tomorrow Jacinto and I will take it back."

Jacinto went to bed that night thinking of Padre
Anton. He was a gringo, a foreigner. Stubborn gringos
had to learn how Mexicans and Indians did things.
Gringos were usually in too much of a hurry. Mostly
they seemed to learn only by pain. And tonight Padre
Anton was unhappy. He sighed in his sleep, although
the mournful sounds could have come from his long
day in the saddle. No, he would never be a rider.
Sometimes he even fell off, but he always got back on
his mule, laughing.

The next morning as Padre Anton and the boy were headed for Gamboa's corral to get mules, they heard a woman's voice calling the priest. Señora Gomez came running across the plaza toward them, waving her arms with excitement. "Padre! Padre!"

Padre Anton stopped. "*Señora,* what is it? Is it Señor Ramirez? Is he ill?"

"No, padre. Tío Carlos sent me to ask you to come to him."

"*Señora,* the day will be very hot, and we want to get an early start. We are going to return the money for the bell. I will come tonight."

"No, no!" she cried. "You must keep the money and give it to Tío Carlos."

"Give it to *him?*" Padre Anton was as thunderstruck by the remark as Jacinto.

"*Sí,* he will make a bell for the church."

"*Tío Carlos will make a bell?*" The priest looked even more astonished.

"In Mexico when he was young he helped make a bell for a church. He says he can do it."

"For twelve dollars?"

"*Sí,* for that, and if you will bring him the supplies he needs."

Shaking his head, Padre Anton started for the Gomez house with Jacinto at his heels.

Tío Carlos had a chair in the corner where El

Cobarde's cage had stood. The old man rose, bowing and grinning when the priest entered.

"You can cast a bell, Tío Carlos?" asked Padre Anton.

"*Sí.*"

The padre looked first at the dirt floor, which the careful housekeeper had swept already that morning, then at the *santos* figure on the wall. He let out his breath, muttering words Jacinto couldn't catch, and asked, "What will you need, *señor?*"

"Much metal, copper, tin—four parts of copper to one part tin. I will need gold and silver also."

Jacinto gasped. "The padre will give you twelve dollars! And you ask for gold and silver, too!"

"I do not mean coins, though they would also melt down. I mean jewelry and silver spoons and shoe-buckles. Silver and gold add tone to a bell."

Padre Anton wanted to know how much copper and tin he needed.

When Tío Carlos told him, the priest looked shaken. He sat down in the old man's chair. "In Yankee measurements that would be a thousand pounds."

"*Sí*, the height of a good bell must be twelve times the thickness of its rim. A fine bell has three tones of music to it. I would like to make a fine bell. I will need other things for the bell—bricks baked hard in a fire, not in the sun, like adobes. Also wet clay, beeswax, fine pieces of wood, and some strips of metal to make a measuring instrument. And some paper, tallow, and of course a large basket of calves' hair."

"Calves' hair!" exploded Padre Anton.

"You will see why I need it. All will see. I will cast the bell on the hillside where the sand is." Tío Carlos pointed first at the hillside, then at Jacinto. "I will want the boy also."

"He will be the easiest of all to donate to you." Padre Anton sounded downcast. "Would you be willing?" he asked Jacinto.

"Sí, padre, if you want me to." Jacinto felt like laughing. Tío Carlos make a church bell? The idea was foolish, but he would humor the old Mexican if doing so would make Padre Anton and Señora Gomez happy. He owed them much. For that matter, he owed much to Tío Carlos for the death of his grandson.

When they'd left the Gomez house, Jacinto drew abreast of the priest. "Some of the people will not like my helping with this bell, padre. I am not a Genizaro. Many say that I bring ill fortune. They say that when the Utes come I am always there to see them. They think my evil draws the Utes."

"They are superstitious children. The Utes have come twice since Agua Mansa was built. Both times they came when the moon was full or nearly so. You have been out of the village twice. It is a coincidence that they came when you were out of the village.

Coincidence happens in life more than most people will
admit. You helped with the new church, and it is fine
and strong, isn't it? This bell, I hope, will be a good
one. If Tío Carlos asks for you, he shall have you. It is
his business. Jacinto, I am more worried about him
than I am about you."

"I am strong. I will lift what I can to spare him,
padre."

"That is not why I worry, Jacinto. Casting of bells
is a very skilled craft. In Europe bell casters work for
many years learning their trade. Whole families are
bell makers. Tío Carlos saw a bell made when he was
young. That was very long ago. I will pray he succeeds.
I see no other way to get a bell for our church."

"I'll work to see that he succeeds," said Jacinto.

"You won't pray, too?"

Jacinto stared at a hen scratching in the dust of the
plaza. "Padre, I am a Comanche. I would lie to you
if I said I was now a Genizaro. I live with you and I
go to Mass, but going to Mass does not touch my heart."

The priest put his hand on Jacinto's shoulder. "You
are honest. If you had been captured as a small boy
like Santos Gamboa, I think you would be a Genizaro
now."

"Sí, padre, I was too old. I remember too much of
my own people."

*   *   *

Quite soon everyone in Agua Mansa realized with surprise that Tío Carlos did indeed know how to cast a bell. The priest, Santos Gamboa, Jacinto, and some of the other men were invited to the Gomez house to examine the drawing of a bell done with charcoal on sheets of paper donated by Joshua Dove. Tío Carlos had glued the sheets together to have enough room on which to sketch the bell to scale. It was to be a good-sized bell, Jacinto thought.

Within the next few days the old Mexican made himself two sets of measuring rods, linked together out of pieces of wood and bits of metal. He showed Jacinto how the legs of the rods curved on the outside to mark the outer rim of the bell. The inside legs marked the inside edge. The space between the sets of legs was to be the thickness of the bell.

"But what am I to do to help you?" asked Jacinto at this point.

"You are to dig a pit of a certain size in the sand of the hillside."

Jacinto shrugged. Collecting the metal proceeded at once, but the work went very slowly. Padre Anton spent all of his time riding about the countryside, this time begging for metal. The mound of old copper pots and kettles and tin pans was growing in the center of the plaza, yet no one could say it was a large pile. The padre received earrings, rings, necklaces, and spoons from women, but there wasn't a great deal of precious metal in them. At this rate casting the bell would take years. Jacinto doubted it would ever happen.

But one day the metal they needed suddenly appeared. An oxcart driven by two Indians from the Aldama ranch arrived unheralded in the plaza. The Indians brought a gift from Don Quirino. It was a small cannon he'd recalled seeing years before, abandoned in the desert. No one knew who had brought it to California, but the cannon was Spanish and so old its date and name had eroded. Padre Anton informed the villagers that Spanish cannon were "named" and the date of their casting was recorded on them. He guessed that some soldiers crossing the desert over a century ago had abandoned it because of its weight.

Tío Carlos was delighted with the cannon. So was Padre Anton, who smilingly said something about "swords being beaten into plowshares."

"What are we going to do with it?" Jacinto asked Tío Carlos.

"Break it up and melt it down with all the other metal. The cannon is brass. Brass is copper, tin, and zinc."

Jacinto helped the settlers attach ropes to the cannon and drag it out of the oxcart.

"Mexicans are mad," the boy told himself, as he watched Tío Carlos tottering happily around the cannon, followed by his old brown dog.

While some of the men of Agua Mansa made adobe bricks and baked them in mud kilns to the degree of hardness Tío Carlos required, others broke up the cannon with sledgehammers. Under the old Mexican's direction they made a deep pit near the small one Jacinto had dug. They lined the deep pit with a double row of bricks set in mortar. The inside row of bricks did not touch the outside row. In a way, Jacinto thought the pit resembled two cooking pots, one set in the other. Tío Carlos said that a fire was to be built between the double walls and fed night and day. When the bricks were hot, he would have the bell metal brought to the hillside and thrown into the pit to be melted down.

But the old man's real attention was given to the pit Jacinto had dug. He sent the boy to fetch his measuring rods one morning. Jacinto returned and found Tío Carlos down in the pit, ramming a stake into the sand. He asked for the rods, then positioned them on the stake where they could pivot.

"Tomorrow we shall lay bricks," he told Jacinto.

Down in the small pit the next day Jacinto helped the old man stuff bricks around the stake, but not so close to it that there wasn't room for a fire to be lit between the bricks and the stake. Men hauled clay in buckets from the riverbank for Jacinto to use over the brickwork. This clay the boy mixed with calves' hair clipped off their spring calves by the amused Aldama *vaqueros*. When they brought it to Tío Carlos, Jacinto noticed how they grinned. They thought he was mad. but as far as they were concerned, all farmers were loco. In fact, the calves' hair was a good binder for the clay, better than straw was for adobes. Then the old man carefully adjusted the inner measuring rod so that the inside shape of the bell was just as he wanted it.

Jacinto smeared tallow and calves' hair over the core of heavy clay, and when the old man was satisfied that the core was perfect, he told Jacinto to put another layer of clay on top of it. This clay was lighter and had no hair binder. Tío Carlos constantly measured this layer to make sure it was equally thick at all points. Finally after many hours of backbreaking work, stooping down to make the shell a little thinner here and a little thicker there, Tío Carlos said he was satisfied. The old man had been a hard taskmaster as he'd made his numberless measurements and given orders to Jacinto to "add a bit here" and "scrape off a bit there."

The New Mexicans wanted their bell named, as was the custom. They had decided among themselves to call it after the Holy Mother, who had appeared long ago to a humble Indian in Mexico. San Salvador, the son of Mary, had his church. Mary would have the bell. Tío Carlos, who could not read or write, asked Padre Anton to write the name Our Lady of Guadalupe and the year on a piece of paper. The old man then molded the name and date in clay, and as the last step in making the light clay layer over the core, had Jacinto press the inscription onto the side of the mold.

At last Tío Carlos was willing to say the light clay covering would do. Jacinto straightened up, relieved, only to hear the old man order, "Now coat all that with tallow and beeswax." Jacinto bent painfully to the new task. With the old man watching closely, he smeared a heavy layer over the light clay. "*Bueno, bueno.* (Good, good.) Now we have only the outer part to do."

Jacinto sagged; his back was a torment from the constant stooping. "So you hurt?" Tío Carlos chuckled. "Are you less than an old man? I hurt, but this must be done and done now. Later we can rest."

Jacinto heaved another sigh and bent again to the old man's orders. Rapidly they built up a thick coat of heavy dark clay, mixed with calves' hair, over the light clay. The old man's constant reminders to "pack it tight," "make it solid," "don't make it too hard," "don't hurt the inner shell" became harsher as Jacinto's back became more painful. But at last the work was done, and the thick outer layer of dark heavy clay pleased the critical old man.

Now Tío Carlos set a fire inside the bricks next to the stake. It baked the clay bell hard in a short time. Through holes in the top of the clay covering Jacinto watched the tallow grease and wax come out as steam. When the covering structure had cooled, Tío Carlos had it lifted off and the clay bell inside it carefully broken up into shards and thrown away. Very carefully Jacinto and the men working with Tío Carlos let the cover down again, leaving an empty but bell-shaped space between the outer clay covering and the core of clay and bricks.

The metal was ready with the unwanted dross skimmed off. In a large iron ladle, which the blacksmith had made, it was brought molten from the melting pit to the bell pit and poured into the mold. Both Jacinto and Tío Carlos stood back to watch. The pouring was no work for a boy and an old man. Working with liquid metal was dangerous, requiring strength, steadiness, and precision. Padre Anton and Santos Gamboa poured most of the metal. For all of his slightness, the priest was strong.

When the men had filled the mold and the top of the covering where they'd poured the metal had been covered with clay, Padre Anton prayed with the settlers, asking God's blessing on their bell. Then he asked, "Tío Carlos, what do we do next?"

"We wait for the metal to cool."

"And how long will that take?" Padre Anton sounded excited.

"Three weeks' time. The larger the bell, the longer it takes to cool."

As he'd worked on the bell, Jacinto often had been too occupied to think. Sometimes, though, when Tío

Carlos had smiled at him, Jacinto felt almost happy. Once the old man said, "Working with you is like being with Teodoro again. We worked well together, he and I. He would have liked to make this bell. He would have wanted our bell."

"Our bell." Jacinto didn't know whether Tío Carlos meant the bell belonged Agua Mansa or Tío Carlos and him. He wanted to think the old man had meant the two of them. He'd learned already that the thing a person worked on belonged even more to him than to the person who was going to receive it or buy it.

But Jacinto never was able to ask Tío Carlos what he had meant. Five days after the metal was poured, the old Mexican died in his sleep. Señora Gomez found him lying in his bed in the morning and came hurrying to Padre Anton.

Jacinto went to Tío Carlos's wake with the other settlers, remembering El Chino's. Few grieved much over so old a man, except to say that it was a great pity he never would hear his bell ring. Señora Gomez cried, promising that she would keep the old man's dog as long as it lived, though it was of little worth and brought fleas into her house.

Everyone in Agua Mansa was flattered, even Santos Gamboa, when Don Quirino came to the wake and attended the funeral Mass. The ranchero even followed the coffin and mourners to the graveyard on the bluff, where Tío Carlos was buried next to his grand-son. After the burial Don Quirino went with the priest and Gamboa to look at the bell pit. Jacinto trailed along as usual after Padre Anton.

"There is nothing to see but clay," Don Quirino said. "Where is the bell? My wife gave the silver buckles from my finest shoes to make it."

Padre Anton pointed. "The bell is inside the clay. In fourteen days' time, the metal will be cool. Then the clay will be removed and the bell taken out."

"What of the clapper?" asked the ranchero.

"Our blacksmith has made one to fit the bell," Santos Gamboa told him. "Before he died, Tío Carlos gave him a drawing."

Jacinto wanted to volunteer the information that Tío Carlos had fashioned a piece inside the bell mold to hold the clapper, but kept silent. He didn't want Don Quirino to notice him and perhaps say something about stealing horses or ask Gamboa how the Comanche boy was behaving.

Don Quirino knelt down and reached out to touch the clay mold. "It is hot."

"It was hotter some days ago," said the priest.

"Who will remove the clay?" asked Don Quirino after he got up.

"The boy here will do it," said Padre Anton.

"This boy? The Comanche Indian?" exclaimed the ranchero.

"*Sí, patrón,*" explained Gamboa. "Tío Carlos chose him. He helped most to cast the bell."

Don Quirino shook his head in disbelief. "Tío Carlos was always a strange man. He could have left Rancho San Bernardino and gone back to Mexico when the Mexican padres left ten years ago. But he stayed on."

"That was probably because all of his family except for his grandson were buried here," explained Padre Anton.

Don Quirino nodded in a thoughtful manner, then asked, "Can the clay be taken off without damaging the bell?" The question was for Jacinto.

The boy said, "*Sí,* the bell is hard. The clay breaks easily." Tío Carlos had spoken to him often about how simply such a thing was done. He'd thought about it a great deal, too, since the old Mexican's death.

But Jacinto did have a worry. He knew that all of the people in Agua Mansa would flock to the hillside to see the mold broken. Don Quirino himself would probably come with his *vaqueros* and perhaps even with the women of his family. What if the bell was not perfect? What if it had a crack in it or, worse, had a piece of the rim broken off or missing? The people would surely say that because the Comanche boy had worked on the bell it had come out wrong. And Tío Carlos wouldn't be at hand to tell them that the flaw was not Jacinto's fault.

The two weeks went by, difficult worried days for

Jacinto, who visited both Ramirez graves daily and left pebbles. On the morning of the day the bell was to be taken out of the pit, he spoke to Padre Anton after Mass. "I am worried about the bell, padre."

The priest was putting on his old sandals, getting ready to go to the hillside. He sat on the edge of his bed and said, "I'm worried, too, Jacinto. Tío Carlos was not a real bell maker. I've prayed that the bell will be a good one. So has everyone else in the village, I suspect. You and Tío Carlos cast it as well as you could, didn't you?"

"*Sí*, padre. We did our best."

"Then no one could do anything more."

"No, padre."

The hillside was thronged with men and women, standing in the blistering September sunlight, when Jacinto went down into the pit with a hammer and a chisel borrowed from the blacksmith. Carefully he chipped at the baked clay. Removing it was as easy as Tío Carlos had said. Clay broke off in great hunks, falling into the pit. Soon Jacinto was knee-deep in shards. Before long the uncovered bell lay under his eyes, yellow in the sunshine.

Jacinto examined it quickly, noticing that the loops to hold the ropes were perfectly cast. He called for the blacksmith and Santos Gamboa to come down into the

pit with the rawhide ropes they had ready. After
threading them through the loops, the men and Jacinto
hauled themselves up out of the pit.

The two men tied the ropes to the yoke of a team
of Don Quirino's strongest oxen and drove them forward. As the heavy bell came up out of the pit, Gamboa
and other strong men steadied its rise with their arms
guiding it.

Then the shouting began as the people saw their
bell for the first time. The glistening, golden-looking
bell was beautiful in their eyes. Jacinto heard the cry,
"It is the bell of San Salvador! See how it shines!"

"No," came the voice of Carmela Gomez. "It is the
bell of Our Lady of Guadaloupe. It is a wonderful,
blessed bell."

The men guided the bronze bell onto a wooden sled
made especially for it to be dragged to the blacksmith's
house. There it would be fitted with a clapper and
then taken to the church on the sled and chained onto
a wooden bar set between two trees.

"Let us hear our bell," a New Mexican from Taos
shouted.

"Let me hear my wife's earrings," said Joshua Dove,
who stood not far from Jacinto.

"And I would like to know how my silver shoe
buckles sound," said Don Quirino, sitting on his horse
next to the sled. Aldama had come with his wife and

daughters, who were dressed in silk and lace but who rode in an oxcart. Almost enough people were present to make the unmolding of the bell a *fiesta*.

Padre Anton called out to Don Quirino. "We have no clapper."

"We have a hammer." Santos Gamboa picked up the hammer Jacinto had set down on the edge of the pit. He handed it to the priest and pointed to the bell on the sled. Padre Anton looked at it for a long moment, then walked up to the bell. He struck it one blow with the hammer.

The sound that came forth wasn't music to Jacinto's ears or to anyone else's. It was a hard, sour, and grating sound, almost painful to the ears. A loud groaning arose from the waiting people.

A woman wailed, "It is a bad bell!"

Padre Anton looked disappointed, too, as he circled the bell with a grim-faced Santos Gamboa. Jacinto saw them stop suddenly and stare at the top of the bell. He hurried over to them and saw the priest stick his fingers into two small holes in the metal near the top. The bell was not perfect. The two holes were the cause of the bad tone.

"Will the bell be good enough for the church?" Gamboa ask the priest.

"It must be good enough. Although it has a sad tone, it is the only bell we can afford, Don Santos. Any bell is better than no bell. It will call the people to

church as well as any other. What a pity that it is a
bad bell!"

Jacinto didn't wait to hear his bell called "bad" a
third time. He spun on his heel and fled up the hillside
toward the cemetery. He was welcome with Teodoro
and Tío Carlos, who had been his true friends. He
could weep there and no one would know.

THE
SANTA
ANA

XII

Jacinto mourned. He had seen the Utes twice and had never harmed them. They had made a fool of him. He had no horse, and he'd brought about the death of his friend. Now, trying to make amends, a thing that had been in the back of his mind since he started the bell, he'd failed completely. Casting a bell with a beautiful voice would have made up somewhat for all the trouble he'd caused. But this bell for the church of San Salvador was a bad one! *Bad* was the only word for its tone.

The Comanche boy didn't watch the blacksmith fasten the clapper inside the bell or file rough places off its surface. He stayed in Padre Anton's house while the New Mexicans brought the bell to the church and

hung it, with a stout chain, on a wooden bar between
the two trees. Jacinto could turn his head away when
he passed the bell, but there was no way to escape its
sound, not when it was placed just outside the church
and the priest's house.

He knew what the settlers were thinking. He could
tell by their hostile faces. A man who was not a Christian should not have helped make a church bell. Such
a person would put a curse on anything that should
be perfect. How could their prayers that the bell be
blessed be heard when Jacinto, a heathen, had worked
with Tío Carlos on it? As for Tío Carlos himself, he
had never come to Mass until he had moved to Agua
Mansa.

The month of October was not as warm as the
previous month. And November first was so cold that
Jacinto had to wear a jacket when he made his daily
visit to the windy bluff where Tío Carlos and Teodoro
lay. As he placed a pebble on Teodoro's pile and one
on his grandfather's, he noticed the food and water
set out in bowls on their graves. Candles would be
brought later and lit on the graves to burn through
the night. Settlers already had come to the priest's
house with gifts of food. It was the evening of All Souls'
Day. Jacinto knew the bell would be rung all night
long, something devout people did to mark the holy
day.

He wouldn't have minded the all-night vigil of the bell half so much if the tone had been perfect. Each sad clang, so different from the beautiful bells of Santa Fe, hurt his ears. The sour note of the bell didn't please Padre Anton either. Jacinto had seen a look of misery on his face sometimes when he was ringing the bell for Vespers.

November continued cold and unpleasant, but no more so than the people of Agua Mansa were to Jacinto. More of them turned their backs and crossed themselves when he went by. A few even spat after him.

Señora Gomez, though, was kind to him. He went to her house when Padre Anton didn't need him and let her stuff him with the kind of food he liked. Padre Anton and Jacinto shared the cooking chores in the priest's house. The padre cooked very strange dishes, in Jacinto's estimation. And the priest claimed that anything cooked by Jacinto had "wildfire" built right into it. The fact was that Padre Anton didn't appreciate red peppers and most likely never would. Too, he didn't seem to like beans every day.

One day early in December while the Widow Gomez was fixing *penocha*, a brown sugar candy, for Jacinto to take as a gift to the priest, she asked, "Do you still think of leaving us, Jacinto?"

"No." Jacinto looked directly at the empty corner that still reminded him painfully of El Cobarde and

Tío Carlos. "I have no horse or mule. I cannot go without an animal to ride. And Don Quirino would have me hunted and killed if I tried to go away."

"That could be true of Don Quirino, Jacinto. He doesn't like you, though I don't see how he could blame you for his son's following the Utes and getting killed by them."

Jacinto laughed bitterly and said, "*Señora,* his shoe buckles are in the bell, and the tone of the bell does not please him."

"So are my silver beads! *Ay de mí,* they were a wedding present. They added nothing at all to the sound of that bell either. My husband put them around my neck the night we were married." The old woman wiped her eyes with her sleeve while she stirred the *penocha* to keep it from scorching. Changing the subject without warning, she said, "People say we will have a cold winter. There is much snow on the mountains."

"I've seen it." Jacinto had thought when he looked at the sharp peaks to the north that the Spanish Trail surely was impassable now.

"Evil things come in threes," Señora Gomez went on. "First, the death of Tío Carlos, then the failure of the bell."

"You've left out the raids of the Utes and the death of Teodoro," Jacinto reminded the old woman.

"Teodoro never lived in Agua Mansa. I speak only

of our village. The six-toed son of the blacksmith has said that a third evil thing will take place before long."

Jacinto said nothing. He knew the blacksmith's youngest son. Many people listened to his prophecies, because Mexicans believed that the deformed and blind could foretell the future. He supposed he should tell Padre Anton of the prophecy, but he decided not to. The Swiss priest had no patience with such things. He'd absolutely refused to give up the key to the church door to a mother who wanted to put it into her daughter's mouth and turn it to the right so the witless child would begin to speak.

Christmas was celebrated at Agua Mansa as it had been in New Mexico, but the sky on Christmas eve was heavy with very dark clouds. While the settlers walked in their procession and went in groups to light tiny Christmas fires on the hillside, they looked up at the mountains where forked lightning flashed again and again. Many cheerful candles burned in the church around the statues of Jesus in his manger and of Mary and Joseph that night at Mass, but the words of Padre Anton sometimes could not be heard for the thunder overhead.

Standing beside the church, Jacinto watched the settlers going home after Mass. The wind tore at the full skirts and trailing *rebozos* of the women. The men had to steady the smaller children to keep them from falling.

Around midnight the rain started. High in the San Bernardino Mountains the same rain turned to snow, making the pack of snow even higher. Rain continued for fifteen days and then all at once stopped. So much rain would make the plain very green in the spring and the desert bloom with many wild flowers, according to Joshua Dove. He came to Agua Mansa one day soon after the New Year with a gift of quail he'd shot for Padre Anton. The old Yankee didn't dismount after he handed the birds to Jacinto.

He looked over the boy's head at the mountains. "There's lotsa snow up in the hills. I heard tell there was three feet of it by Christmas. Now there's plenty more."

"Sí, there has been much rain, Don Joshua. Padre Anton said he thought for a while Noah would get busy if he lived here."

"Well, we're all right now, Jacinto," said the old hunter, looking around at the dazzling sunshine. "It's clear as a bell here." He gave the bell hanging between its trees a strange glance and rode off as if he was embarrassed by his words. It was the first time Jacinto had ever seen him flustered. The sound of the bad bell reached Dove's house all too well.

*   *   *

Sleep didn't come as easily to Jacinto as it once had. Serving Padre Anton wasn't as tiring as shepherding goats and sheep. Brooding so much over his troubles kept Jacinto awake many nights long after Padre Anton was asleep. The boy would lie in his blankets on top of the pile of skins set on the floor, listening to the priest breathing and sometimes speaking in his sleep in a language that was not Spanish.

One night toward the end of January Jacinto couldn't get to sleep at all. The day had been a warm one, so warm and sunny that women had gone about without wrapping themselves in their *rebozos*. But by sunset the northern sky had changed to a gray. The air had been heavy and difficult to breathe that evening. Neither Jacinto nor Padre Anton had any appetite for supper. Later it had started to rain in great warm drops.

Jacinto lay with his arms folded under his head, staring at the darkness of the ceiling while he listened to the rain. He thought of Black Hoof, wondering whether the Utes had killed and eaten him. He hoped not. He hoped they rode the pinto. Comanches considered killing a horse the equal of killing a Comanche. As for Utes, how Jacinto regretted not putting a Comanche arrow into one! He was no warrior of his people. For the thousandth time he thought of Teodoro's horse, Elena. She had disappeared totally—saddle, bridle, and all. The raiders must have driven her off, too.

The boy groaned quietly and rolled over on his side. Because the hides slipped under his body, he rolled onto the floor. It had happened many times before. Jacinto didn't hurry back onto the hides; the dirt was cool on his cheek. For a long while he didn't move, then suddenly he shifted his position and pressed his ear to the dirt, listening.

An instant later he was scrambling out of his blankets. He groped for the candlestick set on top of the chest by Padre Anton's bed, got hold of the tinder and flint next to it, and lit the candle. "Padre, padre!" he cried.

The priest came awake swiftly. As a priest, he was used to being awakened at night to visit the dying and take them the Sacred Heart. "What is it?"

"I don't know what it is!" Jacinto felt foolish through his alarm.

"Is someone in the village dying?"

"No, padre. It's a sound I heard."

"What kind of sound?"

"I don't know. I never heard such a sound before. It came from the ground."

"The *ground*?" Padre Anton threw off his blankets with a jerk. He flopped down onto the dirt in his nightgown, pressing his ear to the floor. Then he was up, swaying. "Holy Mother of God, it is roaring," he whispered. "Ring the bell, Jacinto. Hurry. *Hurry, Jacinto!*"

"Do you know what it is?"

"Yes. *Hurry*. Ring the bell. It will bring the people to the church."

Forgetting that he still held the candlestick, Jacinto ran out into the rain. The wind that had just come up blew out the candle before Jacinto could reach the bell. He dropped the candlestick and found the bell rope. He threw his weight onto it and the bell clanged obediently, tolling hoarsely out over the river.

Jacinto watched points of light appear behind the cowhide shutters of windows. He could imagine the shouting as doors opened and men called back and forth to each other, asking if the Utes had come again. But the boy could hear nothing but the bell as he went on hauling at the rope. People were hurrying up to the church. A few settlers carried torches; by their light Jacinto could see their faces. All looked strained and frightened. Some were crying out to each other or to their children, but Jacinto could not hear what they were saying because of the clamor of the bell.

Last of all he saw Señora Gomez coming up the slope, being helped by another woman.

And then the great rumbling started, so loud that it swallowed up even the sound of the bell. It rose to a thundering roar as the boy let go of the bell rope and turned to stare at the source of the noise, the Santa Ana.

A woman pointed to the north, screaming. Another sank to her knees, her arms around her children.

Jacinto was unaware of the cry he strangled in his throat. The *river*! A monstrous wave of water, several times higher than the church, came raging down the Santa Ana. It roared past beneath their feet, tearing large cottonwoods and sycamores out by their roots, sweeping them along like bits of kindling. Other huge waves followed the first one, rumbling down between the east and west bluffs.

People watched, some sobbing and shrieking, but most in horrified silence, as the flood filled the valley and covered the homes they'd left only minutes before.

"What is it, padre?" Santos Gamboa asked the priest, as the two men stood together next to the bell, watching the wild water. "Will it come up to the top of the bluff?"

"No, Don Santos. The worst of the waves have passed. The warm rain melted the snow in the mountains too quickly," explained Padre Anton.

"We have lost everything. Our animals will have drowned," Gamboa said calmly. Jacinto was proud of the man's restraint. He behaved like a Comanche even if he was a Genizaro.

"We have lost everything but our lives. Everyone was saved." By the light of a torch flickering in the rain, Jacinto saw the priest's face. He was smiling. Padre Anton lifted up his hands. "We shall pray and give thanks for our deliverance from the water."

Jacinto, who stared fascinated at the rushing water,

didn't listen closely to Padre Anton's words. But when he heard his own name, he began to pay heed.

"Jacinto Delacruz, the Comanche, not only was first to hear the noise of the flood's coming, but he and Tío Carlos cast the bell that saved you. Theirs is not a bad bell, as you say. It is a blessed bell. Jacinto has saved the lives of everyone here!"

No kneeling settler turned his head to look at the boy leaning against one of the trees that supported the bell. Padre Anton didn't mention him again. He went on praying as if he'd paid no tribute either to Jacinto or the bell. Jacinto knew that no one would ever speak to him about the words of the priest. But neither would any settler ever forget them! Jacinto Delacruz would never be loved, because he refused to become a Genizaro, but he would be accepted in Agua Mansa if he chose to be. A weight lifted from him. He thought of Tío Carlos. How proud he would have been to know that their bell had done something so important!

By morning only the church and the priest's house on high ground remained intact in Agua Mansa. The other houses either were carried away by the floodwaters or their adobes were melting. Only Santos Gamboa's chimney stood looking like a finger pointing accusingly at the blue sky. All riverside trees were gone, and the fields were covered with gravel and sand that the flood had washed over them. Battered tree branches carried down from the mountains kept sweeping along the course of the Santa Ana. The river had subsided, but it still overran its old channel and now flowed more swiftly.

Jacinto walked about with a melancholy priest and Santos Gamboa. *Sí*, everything was gone, even the animals, except for some mules that had broken down their corral and escaped. They came running to greet the men, nuzzling them, hoping for food. Neither Padre Anton nor Gamboa spoke a word until Joshua Dove came riding up to them, after fording the river, dodging driftwood. "I been to Don Quirino's place. I seen what happened last night from the other side o' the Santa Ana. That bell o' yours fetched me over here. Don Quirino's sendin' a oxcart of grub fer you folks. It'll be here by noon. He's sent a *vaquero* to Don Pedro to tell him to round up clothes and other stuff."

"*Gracias*, Don Joshua," said Gamboa.

"Who guessed the flood was comin' and gave the alarm?"

"Don Joshua, it was Jacinto," said the priest.

The old Yankee nodded. "Well, there's somethin' to be said for ya after all, huh?" He asked Gamboa, "What're you folks goin' to do now?"

"Find shelter and food, then dig new irrigation ditches. We will rebuild and plant our fields."

"Sure you will," Dove said admiringly. "You got grit."

When Dove had left, Jacinto was sent by Padre

Anton to see what he could salvage downstream. He found boards, kettles, pans, and sodden clothing, and he piled everything on high ground for the settlers to sort over later. To his joy three goats and four sheep somehow had escaped alive. They came to their old shepherd when he called. Jacinto led them back to Agua Mansa, delighted that he had good news to go with the bad that Gamboa's white mare lay drowned in the river.

Jacinto arrived to find Don Quirino's cart being unloaded and the supplies portioned out to the settlers. The ranchero, himself, had come to see the damage. He stood talking with Gamboa and Padre Anton. All three men looked as grave as they had when Jacinto had been brought up before old Don Pedro.

A goat came running to the priest, demanding attention. Padre Anton patted it; then, looking up, he saw Jacinto with the other animals. He asked, "Jacinto, Señor Gamboa is not your *patrón*, is he?"

"He says he isn't."

"And I am not," agreed Gamboa.

"Gamboa, you were given no paper for this boy in Santa Fe?" demanded Don Quirino.

"No."

The ranchero turned chilly eyes on Jacinto. "I am told you gave the alarm last night."

"*Sí, patrón.*"

"And you helped cast the bell?"

"*Sí*, you were there when I broke the mold!"

Don Quirino shrugged his shoulders. "I am not your *patrón* either, though you have called me that once or twice, as I recall. You may do as you wish—as long as you touch no horse of mine again."

Jacinto opened his mouth in surprise. What was this about horses? Talking of stealing horses at a time like this! Talking about him!

"Jacinto does not need to steal a horse," said Padre Anton. "I will speak to the traders about him."

Jacinto looked from face to face. What traders? There were no traders anywhere he could see.

"I think Joshua Dove will give him a mule and a colt," added Gamboa. "He told me last week he would do this."

"In return for what? Why would Dove do that for the boy?" snapped Don Quirino.

Padre Anton told him very solemnly, "In return for my not trying to make a good Roman Catholic out of him. Don Joshua understands Jacinto better than I'd thought. He admires his honesty and his stubbornness. Don Joshua's wife wants her husband to join our church." Jacinto knew that Padre Anton was laughing inwardly at the ranchero.

Don Quirino glowered at the priest, shook his head, then turned to Santos Gamboa and spoke about the

river. Would it continue to flow so fast? Would it be
wiser to build the village elsewhere?

"What were they talking about before I came up?"
Jacinto asked Padre Anton.

"You. Do you want to go east with the Santa Fe
traders in April?"

"Will Don Santos and Don Quirino let me go?"
Jacinto asked wonderingly.

"They say they will. You yourself heard Don Quirino agree."

Jacinto looked hard at the priest. No, he wasn't smiling. And he wasn't making a joke as he just had with
Don Quirino. The boy turned his head to stare at the
rushing Santa Ana and at the people of Agua Mansa
bending and stooping as they hunted through the dry-
ing gravel and mud for their possessions. He didn't
need to look behind him at the priest's house below
the bluff and at the cemetery on top of it. The graveyard wouldn't mean so much to him from now on,
though he'd still make his pilgrimage to the graves each
day. He gazed again at the mourning settlers by the
river.

"Padre, if the village is rebuilt by April, I will go
away with the traders."

"And if we can't make adobes fast enough to rebuild
by then, Jacinto?"

"Then, I will stay until another April."

"Is that the Comanche way?" asked the priest.

Jacinto shook his head. "No, a Comanche would never help rebuild a village for Genizaros."

"Whose way is it then?"

Jacinto flushed, but he said the words all the same. "It is your way, padre, and the way of Don Santos, though I will always be a Comanche."

"*Gracias*," said the priest. "I understand."

AUTHOR'S
NOTE

A highly romantic legend has grown up in this century regarding the Days of the Dons, the period in which the action of this novel takes place. This era of California history lasted for only a very brief time, from roughly 1834 to 1848. It did not produce Spanish California as many people think, but Mexican California. Southern California then was not the land of gay *caballeros*, flashing-eyed *señoritas*, and tinkling guitars. It was a harsh land with a harsh society wherein the *patrón* was the all-powerful ruler of an empire of Indian *vaqueros* and servants little better than slaves. Many of the powerful Mexican *rancheros* scarcely could read and write and often depended on American agents to handle their affairs. Because of their naïveté in business matters, the *rancheros* gradually lost out after the Treaty of Guadalupe Hidalgo in 1848 to American newcomers who were better businessmen.

Where does this romantic legend derive from? It comes from novels written for adults in the early part of this century and

247

in the late nineteenth century. They have conveyed the idea of fandangos, *fiestas*, and joyous Indians, happy to have traded their former free lives for the "enlightened" rule of first the Spaniards, then the Mexicans. The Indians were seldom well treated—even, alas, at the California missions. The truth is that Southern California then was a land of outlaws, raiders, and *matanzas*, which strewed the plains with animal carcasses. Except that it was probably even more brutal, Southern California had more in common with old Texas than with Spain.

When the word *pioneer* comes to mind, just about everyone today thinks of covered wagons and the Oregon Trail. They certainly don't think of Indians in any sense of voluntary westward movement. But a party of New Mexicans came to what is now San Bernardino County in the early 1840's to serve as a fighting force for the Mexican *rancheros* against raiding Utes, Mohaves, and Yumas. The New Mexicans were almost entirely of Indian blood themselves, though because they were Genizaros they had Spanish names and were Christians. Some of them were Comanches, captured as children in raids by other tribes and sold as servants in New Mexican towns. A slave trade in Indian children flourished in the far West in the mid-nineteenth century. For all practical purposes these captives lived in peonage, another name for slavery. Quite a few were freed in time by their masters, such as my character, Santos Gamboa. Gamboa is a fictional person, but he is based on the real-life stalwart Comanche, Lorenzo Trujillo, who led the New Mexicans to Rancho San Bernardino as settlers. Trujillo died in 1855.

The New Mexicans came to California over the Old Spanish Trail. Unlike the Oregon Trail, it no longer exists as a marked road. Parts of it still can be traveled only by muleback. Other easier routes to California replaced it in the 1850's. I have attempted to describe the Old Spanish Trail as John C. Fremont, the noted explorer, and others wrote of it.

The history of Agua Mansa, the historical community, is

actually more complicated than I have made it in this novel. The true events mentioned in *The Bad Bell of San Salvador* took place in a period of over twenty years from 1843 to 1866. Because this is a book for young readers and I can scarcely have Jacinto grow from age thirteen to his mid-thirties, I've had to telescope time, juggle chronology, and cram all events into a little over two years' time during the Days of the Dons. But I've tried to give an accurate picture of this period of California history, one that is not overcolored by romance.

Briefly, this is the accurate chronology (for those who might be interested).

The land-hungry New Mexicans came for riverfront fields donated by a family of prominent Mexican *rancheros* in 1843 or 1844 (the date is uncertain). They settled beside the Santa Ana River, naming their first village La Placita. Their first church was built here in 1852 after California became part of the Union. Built on quicksand, it collapsed totally just before it was finished.

The people didn't stay at La Placita. They moved across the Santa Ana and built a new adobe village, which they called Agua Mansa. There the devout New Mexicans built a church dedicated to San Salvador, the Holy Savior, and this time they built safely on high ground.

Though their church had no bell tower, the Agua Mansa villagers had a bell. As a matter of fact, two bells are associated with Agua Mansa. I've combined their stories for this book. The first bell, which hung between two trees, wasn't much as bells go, and it didn't last long. But its pealing saved the lives of the settlers during the terrible flood of January, 1862. By 1866 this bell had cracked and become useless. The priest at the time decided there should be a new one. He found it impossible in his impoverished parish to collect the needed sixty dollars, so another bell was cast near Agua Mansa by an "old Mexican" for the sum of twelve dollars with the people supplying the metal. This second bell, a rather crude but touching effort, was dedicated to Our Lady of Guadalupe. It came out of the mold flawed. To the villagers, who had hoped for something melodious, the tone of the homemade bell was unpleasant. In a time of financial trouble, years later, the bell was sold by the parish of San Salvador. Minus its clapper, it was removed from the second church (which eventually fell into ruin), taken away from Agua Mansa, and embedded in concrete as a curio in the patio of the Mission Inn Hotel in Riverside, California. (Because of the encompassing cement I couldn't gauge the quality of the bell's tone, something it is said "no living person has heard.")

Although houses were rebuilt, Agua Mansa never really recovered from the flood of 1862. The Spanish-speaking people, who had rather ill-defined title to their lands, ran into legal difficulties with Americans over property rights. Battling the prejudiced, prosperous, and legally canny Americans was impossible for many settlers. They gradually deserted Agua Mansa. Eventually the descendants of the New Mexicans were absorbed into Mexican-American communities throughout the area. The surnames of the original New Mexicans dot the telephone books of Riverside and San Bernardino Counties today.

Some readers might be interested in the casting of the bell. Though I have no historical evidence to support it, I suspect that the bell was cast in the manner described. My research informed me this procedure was how unsophisticated craftsmen made church bells at one time.

Today only the bell-in-cement, the ruins of the church foundations, and the graveyard on the bluff remain of the village of Agua Mansa. But not quite all, though the last relic is a bit less substantial. The ghost of a girl supposedly walks the old road beneath the bluff and has been "seen" recently by several people. But hers is another story.

Certain characters in this book are modeled on actual historical personages.

One is Joshua Dove, who is based on Isaac Slover, a Kentuckian noted for his skill hunting bears, which he called "cabibs." An old mountain man, Slover was killed in 1854 by a grizzly. Legend has it that he was a good friend of the New Mexican people of Agua Mansa. The tale goes that he was first buried with Protestant rites, but his Catholic wife had Catholic services said for him, too, and had his body removed to the Agua Mansa cemetery. Old-time residents of the Colton-San Bernardino-Riverside area claim to have seen Slover's grave marker, though because of vandalism or neglect it is no longer visible.

Padre Anton was not a real person, though as a Swiss priest he would not have been historically unlikely at Agua Mansa. The first priests who went there were not Mexicans but Europeans.

The Aldama family is based on the Lugos, the owners of Rancho San Bernardino until 1851, when it was sold to Mormon settlers. My Don Pedro Aldama, head of the family, has as his prototype, Don Antonio María Lugo, one-time mayor of the pueblo of Los Angeles. Don Quirino is based on Don José del Carmen Lugo, who was born in 1813 and was the son of Don Antonio María. José del Carmen Lugo had several sons, none of them nicknamed El Chino.

Fiestas at the Lugo ranch house, which still stands on the outskirts of the city of Redlands, were famous, though the entertainments would not be pleasant to average American tastes today. There was a bullring made of adobes with seats on the top. Wild bulls were fought in it. Bull-and-bear fights also were held there—with the bull tied to the bear. Horse races and rooster-buried-in-the-ground games were common parts of the festivities.

Cockfighting was a favorite activity of the Mexicans in California during the 1840's. Because the sport is illegal today, information about it is hard to come by. I cannot reveal my sources, though I might say that this research was slower in materializing than I'd hoped for, since some of my informants were serving longish jail terms for their devotion to the sport.

The California *vaquero* was acknowledged the "best in the West," even by grudging Texans. He was not only a superb horseman but an artist with the lariat. Today the *charros* of Mexico, "gentleman riders," keep up many of the skills of the old-time *vaqueros* and wear a version of the same costume.

The Ute Indians were the terror of Southern California *rancheros* in the 1840's and 1850's up to the death of their fierce chief, Walkara, in 1855. A very warlike people, the Utes were sometimes joined by renegades from other tribes and by white men. Utes ran off California horses, not so much because they valued them as mounts but because they were easier to drive than steers and to Ute taste were just as delicious.

And speaking of horses, Huechino was a real horse of some renown. I could not learn what he looked like but decided that if I had to use a *reata* and play a grizzly, I'd want a small quick horse, not a cumbersome animal.

Although the Comanche Indians enter this story only as transplanted people, I've tried to make Jacinto a true Comanche in his religious beliefs and attitudes. The weapons he fashioned would have been recognized as Comanche-made. Riding in a sort of sling was a Comanche specialty. So was breaking horses in a river where the water cushioned a rider's fall and exhausted the horse.

On the other hand, Teodoro's method of catching a wild horse was the accepted Mexican way, as was the horse-breaking process of twisting the horse's neck to one side, then the other.

Quite a number of books were read in the course of the six-year research for *The Bad Bell of San Salvador*. The most important of them were: *Heritage of the Valley* by George and Helen Beattie; *Old Spanish Trail* by LeRoy R. and Ann W. Hafen; *History of San Bernardino Valley from the Padres to the Pioneers* by Father Juan Caballeria; *La Vida de un Ranchero* by José del Carmen Lugo; *History of San Bernardino and Riverside Counties* by John Brown, Jr., and James Boyd;

Pioneer Notes by Judge Benjamin Hayes; and *A Colony for California* by Tom Patterson.

Much of my San Bernardino County local history came from newspaper files of the *Riverside Press-Enterprise* and *San Bernardino Sun*. Librarians were very kind to photocopy material for me. As always, I owe them much gratitude.

So many people helped me in the course of writing this book that I must regretfully list them alphabetically. Some are librarians; others are people interested in old Agua Mansa and the history of Southern California. They are: Betsy Abel, Mary Caldwell, Dr. Carlos Cortés, Charles Field, Zoma Henry, Carmelita Francesca Reyes de Keown, Oscar Lewis, Ernest Lopez, Donald Miller, Tom Patterson, Mary Ann Selkirk, Dorothy Smith, Colonel A. Stevens, and Father John F. Wagner.

In particular, however, I wish to thank Dr. Myra Ellen Jenkins, archivist of the State of New Mexico, for helping me with research concerning New Mexico not only in 1969 when I first met her, but for replying so courteously and promptly to inquiring letters and long-distance calls since then.

Only one other thing remains to be said: the Santa Ana River exists today, though barely. It's now mostly a dry riverbed with pools here and there, proving the presence of water underground. The Santa Ana is not always dry, however. In winters of heavy snows in the mountains it still flashfloods and creates damage. It never has been totally tamed!

Patricia Beatty
August, 1972

Now a resident of Southern California, Patricia Beatty was born in Portland, Oregon. She was graduated from Reed College there, and then taught high-school English and history for four years. Later she held various positions as science and technical librarian. Recently she taught Writing Fiction for Children in the Extension Department of the University of California, Los Angeles. She has had a number of historical novels published by Morrow, several of them dealing with the American West in the 1860 to 1895 period.

Mrs. Beatty has lived in Coeur d'Alene, Idaho; London, England; and Wilmington, Delaware, as well as on the West Coast. Her husband, Dr. John Beatty, her co-author for a number of books, teaches the history of England at a major California university. One of their books, *The Royal Dirk,* was chosen as an Award book by the Southern California Council on Children's and Young People's Literature. The Beattys have a teen-age daughter, Ann Alexandra.

DARIA